As he approached home, Brian wondered how his mother would be—tense and irritable, or worse—all blurry and sloppy with the wet rings of beer cans on the table and her eyes staring at the television, unfocused. The cans had been piling up in the trash the past week, and he had a feeling that's how she would be today. When she was drinking, she got really angry if he squabbled with Andy.

Andy. Brian kicked a bottle in the street and felt disappointment when it didn't break. His younger brother seemed to be all the things Brian wasn't— tough and wide awake and good at baseball and fights and getting what he wanted. Especially from her. Especially when she was drinking her beer . . .

"The author of *It's Like This, Cat* has created another deeply empathic portrait that is saddening in its realism but heartening as an expression of faith in human nature."

—(starred review) *Booklist*

"A masterpiece."

—*Catholic Library World*

EMILY CHENEY NEVILLE has written several novels for young adults, including *It's Like This, Cat*, which won the Newbery Medal. A graduate of Bryn Mawr College, Ms. Neville taught for two years in the St. Louis public school system, during which time she gathered material and ideas for *Garden of Broken Glass*. She currently lives in upstate New York.

THE LAUREL-LEAF LIBRARY brings together under a single imprint outstanding works of fiction and nonfiction particularly suitable for young adult readers both in and out of the classroom. The series is under the editorship of Charles F. Reasoner, Professor of Elementary Education, New York University.

Garden of Broken Glass

Emily Cheney Neville

Published by
Dell Publishing Co., Inc.
1 Dag Hammarskjold Plaza
New York, New York 10017

Laurel-Leaf Library ® TM 766734,
Dell Publishing Co., Inc.

ISBN: 0-440-92773-0

Reprinted by arrangement with Delacorte Press
Printed in the United States of America
First Laurel-Leaf printing—January 1979

chapter
one

"SEE THAT COOL leather hat that cat
had for five dollars? I goin get me one." Dwayne
tipped his head as if the hat were already on
it.

"Where you gettin five dollars?" Melvita said.

"Girl, can't you keep yo ole evil mind off
money for even one minute?" Dwayne let the
grocery cart he was pulling thud to a stop.
"Here. They yo groceries. You pull 'em up this
big hot hill!"

Melvita grabbed the cart as if it didn't weigh
a thing and started up the hill at high speed.

Behind, Dwayne grinned and whistled apprecia-
tively. It didn't really bother him that she was an
inch taller than he. No one was going to mess
with Melvita and come out winners. He watched
approvingly as her big legs pumped up the hill
and the orange yarn in her hair bobbed like a
signal.

He yelled, "You be one fine-lookin chick pullin
that cart. I really dig you!"

At the top of the hill she thumped the cart
down on its legs and waited for him to amble up.
"O.K., boy, it be on the level now—you go on an
pull it."

"Can't make me mad. No way. Remember,
you goin to buy me a soda, after I get yo groceries home."

They were at the corner of Twelfth Avenue,
on the near southside of St. Louis. They looked
back downhill at the Mississippi River, limp and
gray under the smog. Boats chugged, trains
rattled over the big bridge, and the Arch rose—
aloof, shiny and golden in the morning sun,
above the smog.

Dwayne said, "It be cool down there in
Soulard. I like to buy a lot of stuff, even if it do
be heavy." He dragged the cart across Twelfth
Avenue and yanked it up the high curb.

Melvita shrugged. "Jus food. Same ole."

"Aw, it ain't all food. You know, they got live
ducks, and jewelry, and leather hats. And those
farmers—they talk funny. Where you think they
come from?"

"Arkansas or someplace. They treat you nice,

though. They ain't mean. You see those glass things, sort of milky glass? I goin get my momma a pink glass swan for Christmas."

"Maybe I get my momma one, too. I goin to have a lot of money by Christmas. Goin to earn a lot of money this summer."

"Yeah, that be good," Melvita said. "Some dudes can't get no job. Where you workin?"

"I ain't decide yet. I see when school get out." Dwayne let the subject drop. "You see that dumb Brian down there in the market? That boy so dumb, he see me every day, and every day he don't reconize me. I have on that leather hat down there, checkin out how it look on me, and I wink at him, and he look at me like I be an ole piece of leather myself. Lookit him now—crawling up the hill behind us like an ole white caterpillar!"

Melvita looked back and laughed. "He ain't bad. He just kinda skinny and dopey. You know —lotta white boys be like that; they just don't reconize people. That Brian, he say 'Hi' to me in school sometime."

Brian was about a block behind them, lagging up the hill in the hot sun behind his skinny shadow. He was in no hurry, and he hadn't bought anything. He just went to Soulard Market Saturday mornings because it was someplace to go, to get out of the house. On lucky days he had a quarter to get popcorn or something, but today wasn't a lucky day.

He saw Melvita and Dwayne ahead of him but made no effort to catch up. He knew Melvita, but then everyone in school knew her. She had a style of her own. She was the best at volleyball and she talked a lot in class and had a lot of friends. But Brian didn't notice much in school. He went just to have a place to go Monday through Friday. His body sat at the desk but his mind was somewhere else. He only knew a few of the kids' names. There was Lionel, a light-skinned boy with a big reddish Afro, who sat beside him. There was fat Martha and big tub Jasper; you couldn't miss them. The only other white boy in the class was Jake, sixteen and almost six feet tall. There were several white girls, but they kept to themselves and thought they were so smart. If they noticed Brian at all, they just giggled. He ignored them.

There were a dozen or so black boys, all about the same size, and Brian never knew which name went to which. He didn't really look at them. He didn't look, because he had a feeling that if he caught a kid's eye, pretty soon the kid would bump him or trip him, or try to get him into a fight some way. It was better not to look.

So he walked up the hill from the market, his eyes squinting down at the sidewalk which gave back heat and dust. He flicked bits of broken glass and trash with his toe. Broken glass seemed to grow in St. Louis like part of the earth. It came from the windows of abandoned houses to begin with. Then since there was so much around already, more windows were broken, more bottles thrown. The crop flourished.

Brian crossed the avenue and looked down toward Lafayette Park. Vaguely he noticed Melvita and Dwayne turn off down a side street before the park, but neither his eyes nor his mind followed them. The park looked cool and dark, a relief from the street. He went in and walked on the grass, then lay down on his stomach on the cool cement beside the fishpond. He sailed sticks around, or just trailed his fingers in the water and watched the patterns. Watching made him sleepy and he moved over onto the grass and dozed off. When he woke up, he was hungry. He lay there looking up at the trees and thought what to do.

Go home? No. Look for a friend? No. He didn't have a friend. Finally he got up, stretched, and ambled over to the little grocery store. The store didn't deliver, but Brian had found, if he stood outside, sooner or later he could get a lady to pay him a quarter for carrying her groceries. Sometimes the lady would even give him a banana or a doughnut from her bag. He always looked hungry.

He got his quarter fairly quickly this time and went back to the store for an ice-cream bar and a pretzel. He wished he had enough for a soda to go with the pretzel, but the water fountain in the park would have to do. After he'd eaten, he went up to Jefferson Avenue to the library and watched an old movie. The librarian was getting

5

ready to close when the movie ended, and Brian knew he'd have to go home now. His feet dragged as he headed toward Rutger Street. His street. Home.

He couldn't remember really wanting to go there ever. Maybe once, when his father still lived with them . . . The idea of his father flickered in his mind, the way a match flicks a spark and then doesn't light. Brian didn't want this idea to light. It was too long ago, and he couldn't remember now how his father looked, or sounded, or acted. There was only a blur, a feeling that once there had been someone, then an ache when he left. . . . Forget it.

But he couldn't forget his mother. She was home, and she drank. Not all the time, of course. Even so, when she wasn't drinking, she got mad at him for some little thing, like letting the screen door slam. Eve said it was nerves. Eve was his older sister, seventeen, and in high school. She had tried to explain it to him once, repeating phrases she'd heard in the health unit on alcoholism.

As he approached home, Brian always wondered how his mother would be, tense and irritable, or all blurry and sloppy with the wet rings of beer cans on the table and her eyes staring at the television, unfocused. The cans had been piling up in the trash the past week, and he had a feeling that's how she would be today. When she was drinking, she got really angry if he squabbled with Andy.

6

Andy. Brian kicked a bottle in the street and felt disappointment when it didn't break. Andy seemed to be all the things Brian wasn't—tough and wide awake and good at baseball and fights and getting what he wanted. Especially from her. Especially when she was drinking her beer. She patted his head and treated him like her baby and thought Brian was picking on him. Huh! Brian let his breath out in disgust. Andy was eleven, not as tall as Brian but almost as heavy. He wasn't any baby, but he said, "Please, Mommie," and got his way like a baby.

When Brian reached his corner, he paused, looking down the street and trying to get himself together. He didn't notice the landmarks of Rutger Street, the burned-out buildings with signs that read These Premises Condemned, the plywood-covered windows chalked with dirty words and half plastered with political posters. He could see his own house, the third one on the block, and see the side porch that opened off the kitchen. No one was sitting there now; there was just some laundry hanging. He moved along, his feet scuffing, his shoulders hunched around him like a turtle shell. His stomach growled. He opened the screen door. It squeaked. It always did that, giving him away.

"Whe-ere you been?" His mother's voice hit him, an angry whine rising over the bleat of the television. She was alone in the kitchen with a bottle of beer in front of her. There were dirty dishes stacked by the sink.

"Just out. Round the park," Brian said.

"Y' can come home, time f' dinner? Think I got nothin' to do, bu' save dinners for yuh?"

Brian edged around the table, wanting to eat but wanting to get out of the room even more. Eve came to the kitchen door, half blocking it, and frowned at him. She didn't see why he couldn't get home on time—it would be one less thing for their mother to get mad at.

He mumbled, "Sorry. I didn't know what time . . ."

His mother shoved her chair back, and the legs shrieked on the linoleum. "Y' don' know! Y' don' know nothin'! Dummy!" She picked up her beer bottle and lurched into the screen door. It opened and she went outside. Brian heard the familiar squeak of the metal chair as she sank into it. Eve let out a short sigh of annoyance and went back into the other room.

Brian looked over at the stove and saw a fly rise from a plate of macaroni with cheese sauce. He got a glass of Kool-Aid out of the refrigerator, sat down, and poured ketchup over his plate. It looked better that way. It didn't taste bad, even if it was cold, and it filled the growling space inside him. He finished and took his plate to the sink. When he put it down, he noticed the other plates had scraps of ham fat left on them. "How come I didn't get any ham?" he said aloud, before he could stop himself.

His mother's shrill, nasal voice hit him, her words getting thicker and more slurred now. "Y' act like an old stray dog, come in any ol' time—

don't 'spect find meat on your plate! You wanta know? Well, y' brother ate it." She laughed suddenly, and the chair squeaked as she bent to reach for her glass.

Brian ate a sandwich of bread and jelly and drank another glass of Kool-Aid. Then he went quietly down the hall to the back yard. Andy was squatting in the yard, fiddling with a broken bicycle. Brian jumped on him from behind and the two rolled over and over in the dirt. Andy was tough, but Brian had caught him by surprise.

"I'll teach you to eat my ham! There—eat dirt!" Brian was on top, and he pushed Andy's face into the dirt.

Satisfied, he relaxed and was caught off guard when Andy reared back up. Andy got him down this time, grabbed his hair, and banged his head against the hard gravel. Stars shot before his eyes. Andy looked at him and then got off warily. Brian staggered up and back into the house. A great wave of sour cheese rose in his throat. He got up the stairs to the bathroom and sat there until his mouth stopped watering. He wiped his cold, sweating hands on his pants and thought dumbly, even Andy can beat me now. He's stronger than me.

Eve came upstairs to use the bathroom, and Brian went and flopped on his bed. He lay there and heard the television droning, and heard voices occasionally. He wondered how he could get out of the house without having to speak to anyone.

After a while he went down the stairs quietly, but his mother was in the kitchen and so was Andy. Eve was washing the dishes.

"Watcha pickin' on him for, you big bully? Putting dirt in his mouth! Com'ere, I'll teach you!" She swayed a little as she yelled at him.

Brian moved around the table. "Tattletale! Why don't you yell at him? He almost busted my head on a rock! Anyway, he's got no right to eat my ham!"

"I didn't eat it all. She took some." Andy nodded at Eve.

Eve said, "I did not take it, smarty-pants. Mother gave it to me."

The words stung. Knowing it was useless, knowing he should just get out, Brian couldn't help arguing. "Why did you give her my food? What's so special about her?"

"She some help round here. Sh' care for someone. Not like you—don' care for no one. Jus ol' stray dog!"

"I saw a dog get run over today. He was all squashed . . ." Andy said.

"Stop it! Don't talk about it!" Eve turned off the water, slammed down a handful of silver, and ran out of the kitchen.

Brian could see his mother trying to focus on him. "Watch out, you! Always making trouble, messy as ol' dog. W'ch out, you get run over, too. . . ." Brian darted for the screen door and was out. "Co' back here! Wanna talk to you!" she yelled.

A bunch of girls from his class were just passing on the street. They snickered as he ran past. Brian didn't care. He ran to the corner, then slowed and walked to the park, his refuge. There was something calm about the green park and the tall narrow houses that looked out on it, with their peaked roofs and shiny black windows. This had once been an elegant part of St. Louis. Most of the houses facing the park were still well kept up, though a few were crumbling, some were boarded up, and there was one bramble-grown vacant lot.

People were afraid to go in the park at night, but it was still light and kids were playing ball, so Brian walked in. Vaguely through his head flitted pictures from the movie he'd seen that afternoon, a movie about surf riders. The waves rolled in, crashed, and the still water ran back and made itself into another wave. Brian thought, you go home and some kind of a wave breaks. Maybe a big wave, maybe just a little one. Then you go away, get yourself back together. He shook his head and wondered what it would be like to swim in all that bubbly, moving water. He'd never swum in anything but the chlorine-smelling, white-tiled pool at the public bath. He rubbed his nose and breathed in deeply —the park smelled moist and fresh and it was quiet. He forgot entirely the smell of beer and macaroni, the angry voices, the snickers. He knew, it had happened so many times before, whatever outbursts there were at home, he could always run away and put them out of his mind.

Finally he noticed that it was getting dark, so he went out on Park Avenue. He saw some girls playing on the sidewalk and walked down that way. A little girl was skipping rope, and the older girl was turning. The other end of the rope was tied to the gate.

He knew the older girl. It was fat Martha, from his class. She laughed a lot, about being fat, or about anything else.

She saw him and sang out: "Hey, Brian, where you hurrying to?"

Standing there flat-footed, Brian said, "Nowhere. I ain't hurrying."

"Ooo-eee! You sure ain't! Move bout as fast as a dead caterpillar!"

"Well, I got no place I want to go right now."

The little girl, who was about five, said, "You want to skip rope with us?"

"Katie, he don't skip rope!"

"Well, he could turn. It work better when two peoples turn. Don't work so good tied to the fence. You want to turn, boy?"

"Ain't you the sassy one!" Martha said.

"I don't mind," Brian said. He untied the rope from the gate, and Martha started swinging. Brian started too late, and the rope flopped on the sidewalk. Katie stamped her foot. "Boy, you don't know how to turn!"

"Boys don't be skipping rope much," Martha said. Brian finally got it going, and Katie started jumping and chanting a rhyme. Someone in the house shouted to Martha and she called back.

"You live there?" Brian asked.

"Sure do. Me and my whole family. That the Houghton Hotel you lookin at!"

"You got a big family?"

"Well, they's me, my momma, my daddy, my gran'ma, my five brothers and sisters, not counting my big sister, she Katie's momma, and . . . oh, I don't know. Some other cousins, they come time somethin go wrong at their house. My momma draw people like jam draw flies."

Brian said, "It must be pretty tough, living with all those people."

"Boy, what you mean, tough! They the sweetest people in the world! Watch it! That's my family you talkin about!"

Brian messed up turning the rope again. "I mean, don't they bother you?"

"Nah! Somebody get mad, holler at the other one, but don't mean nothin. That's *famlee*—you don't get along with your own family, boy, you don't be getting along!"

"I hate my family."

The words floated there, over the dusty evening street. Martha's arm stopped turning, and she and Katie stared at Brian. "Boy, don't talk foolish! So maybe you had a fight, but you know you love your momma."

"I hate my mother the most of all."

Katie drew in her breath sharply and covered her mouth. "O-o-o, he talk bad!" she said.

"White boy, you quit talkin crazy like that round here! Go long home; me and Katie can manage this rope! Don't need yo kind of help. Come on, Katie, baby."

"I'm sorry. I didn't mean nothing," Brian said. His hands hung limp as Martha twitched the rope out of them.

"You don't mean nothin, don't say nothin!" she snapped. "Here, Katie, we skip together." She swung the rope over both their heads and joined Katie, singing, "Hurray, hurray, hurray, sir. What you doing today, sir? Catching polar bears, sir. . . ."

They skipped and counted polar bears up to nineteen, and then stopped, panting and giggling. Brian leaned against the fence, looking down at the sidewalk.

Martha said, "Boy, cheer up—I ain't goin to stay on your case all night. What the trouble over to your house? Who you fight with?"

"I had a fight with my brother, but that was nothing much. It's my mother. She don't pick on the others the way she does on me. She calls me an old stray dog, and dumb and everything."

"Few bad names don't hurt—they call me Fatty all the time."

"Well, you are . . . sort of, I mean . . ." Brian fumbled.

"Go ahead, you can say it. I is fat, I know it! And what you mean, you *ain't* dumb, that it?"

"Uh . . . well, I dunno. Just anything I do, it's wrong."

"I don't know if you act home the way you do in school. You may not *be* dumb, but you sure *act* that way most times. You always be lookin out the window, readin the wrong book."

"Oh, that."

"Yeah, that! And you don't hardly talk to no one. Tell me, who your best friend, huh?"

"No one particular."

"No one at all, that who! Cause you don't try to be friendly. Why, you never even speak to me before, in school."

"I just didn't see you."

"O-o-o-ee! First time anyone say they don't see fat Martha!"

"Well, you know what I mean."

"Reason you don't *see* is cause you don't *look*! Now Monday morning, you come into school, and you see me, and you *look*, hear? You can even say somethin."

"O.K."

"I might even walk home with you after school."

"O.K."

"That all you can say, 'O.K.'? You afraid someone laugh at you, walkin along with fat Martha?"

"Unh-unh, I don't care," Brian said. "I don't want to get in fights, though. I mean, like you got a boy friend that would get mad, or anything?"

Martha sniffed. "Ain't nobody ownin fat Martha! I walk with whom-so-ever I please! Come on, Katie, time us went in. See you Monday—and I mean, *see*!"

"I'll see you," Brian said.

chapter
two

BRIAN WENT TO SCHOOL Monday morning as if he were expecting something to happen. He felt different. He got in line in the yard beside Lionel.

"Hi!" he said. "What's doing?"

Lionel stared. "Man, you is awake! What happen—your momma pour cold water over your head?"

Brian smiled. "No, I just woke up."

They went upstairs to the classroom, and instead of staring out the window as usual, Brian kept glancing at the door. The girls' line hadn't come up yet.

Then they came, whispering, giggling, fingering each other's hair ribbons. Fat Martha heaved in the door, panting from the two flights of stairs and leaned against a desk. Brian caught her eye and said, "Hi!" but hardly out loud.

Martha shouted across the room to him: "Hey, Brian! Why don't you tell the man to cancel school? It be too hot!"

Other kids picked it up. "Yeah, Brian, you tell him!" They laughed and slapped and play-punched each other.

"All right, ladies and gentlemen, in your seats!" Mr. Cousins, their homeroom teacher, had a way of talking rather formally to noisy students, and it worked. At other times he dropped easily into street language to settle a fight between two dudes, or to turn off the fat jokes directed at Martha or Jasper. There was no question of getting any real work done in June— the books had been returned to the storeroom, and the street noise poured in the open windows.

When Brian got outside after school, he saw Martha in the middle of a bunch of girls, all talking at once, moving down the sidewalk. Brian crossed the street slantwise, so he came out a little ahead of the girls, on the other side of the street.

"Hey, Brian, wait up! You goin buy me that soda?"

"Uh, sure," Brian said, listening to the other girls giggle as Martha crossed the street. He fingered his empty pockets and added, "I got to go home first."

"Bye, seeya tonight!" Martha called to the girls, and to Brian she said, "You don't got to buy me no soda. We goin home and gettin it for free out of the icebox."

At the corner they walked past a bunch of boys waiting to get a ballgame together. Brian heard chuckles and a wolf whistle. He pretended not to hear. But Martha stopped dead, her hands on her hips. "What you say, there, boy? Speak up—fat Martha want to hear you!"

"I just clearin my throat. I got me a cold," the boy sputtered. The other boys laughed, slapped their legs, and ran.

"I clear your throat for you, boy. Come long, over here!" He ran, too, and Martha walked easily along beside Brian again. "Don't let 'em take an inch, that what fat Martha say, and that what she do!"

"They're always making those . . . you know, fat jokes in school. Doesn't it make you sore?"

"I don't pay no mind to that. Except old Jasper, he so fat himself, he make me sick with his big mouth and his melon belly!"

Brian thought about it and realized that Martha and Jasper, the two biggest kids in the class, usually started the fat jokes about each other. He'd always laughed along with the others. He wondered now, did they mind, really?

They walked down Park Avenue and turned in at Martha's house. The yard was cluttered with toys, whole and broken. Katie ran to

Martha, and a baby boy toddled over and hung onto her leg.

"Leggo! I gotta get me a cold drink!" Martha said.

Katie looked at Brian. "You coming in my house?"

"Uh-huh."

"You goin to live here?"

Martha laughed. "Katie, you silly! He ain't goin to live here—he got his own family."

"He don't like them."

"You remember that!" Martha shook her head. "Well, he ain't livin here, he jus gettin a cold drink."

They walked into the house, and Martha led the way into the kitchen and opened the icebox. "Momma, this here is Brian. Brian, my momma."

She pulled out a pitcher, poured two glasses full of a purple drink, and drank most of hers in a few gulps.

Her mother said, "Girl, why you gotta drink standing up like a horse? Here, Brian, sit down, make yourself comfortable."

Martha refilled her own glass and flopped into a chair. "I don't know why they even have school in June. It wear me down!"

"You lucky you have school so many months. Didn't used to."

Mrs. Houghton looked at Brian. "How you get along in school, Brian? You work hard?"

"Yes, ma'am."

"You try to do what the teacher tell you, right?"

"He try to see what be out the window," Martha said. "He don't even hear the teacher, less Lionel poke him."

"You daydreaming, Brian?" Mrs. Houghton said. "How you goin to get to high school that way?"

"I gonin!" Martha said. "I wish I be there now. No sense hangin round that old Clinton School no more."

Mrs. Houghton said, " 'Gonin'—what kind of word is that? You won't be going nowhere, you talk like that."

"Momma, I got to talk natural at home. You ought to hear me—I talks real nice to the teacher all day."

"You got brothers and sisters in school, Brian?" Mrs. Houghton asked.

"My sister's in high school."

Mrs. Houghton smiled approvingly. "She get herself a good job, that way. Teach, work in a bank, most anything. What line of work your daddy in?"

"He don't live with us."

Mrs. Houghton talked on easily. "I'm sorry. Martha, I thank the Lord you got one fine father. He always home, every night. Now, how bout you takin' your friend outside, keep an eye on those babies for me?"

On her way out, Martha stopped to get a box of doughnuts. "I need this like a dog need a chain," she said, biting into one. "Here, Brian, have one."

They sat outside on the step and played cards for a while, and then they turned the rope for Katie to skip. Brian looked up, and there was his brother Andy walking down the sidewalk, swinging his baseball mitt.

"Whatcha doing?" Andy said.

"Turning a rope, what's it look like?" Brian said.

Andy glanced at Martha, then passed his glove over his face to hide a smirk. He went on down the street. Brian frowned.

"Who that?" Martha asked.

"My kid brother."

"Who else in your family you haven't told me about?"

"No one. I already told you about Eve."

"She pretty?"

"Nah . . . I don't know. She's fussy. Always crabbing about me leaving a mess in the bathroom, or something."

"You share a bathroom, you got to pick up yo mess, boy, that stand to reason. Why don't you try and get long with your family, stead of findin fault?"

"Oh, Eve's all right, I guess. It's just . . . I can't explain. If you saw my family, you'd see."

"I come over yo house one day, O.K.?"

Brian looked down and felt himself blushing. Martha laughed. "That tickle me, see a white boy blush!" Then her voice changed abruptly. "Your momma don't like colored, huh?"

Brian was startled. He hardly knew himself

that that was what he was thinking. He said, "When she's in one of her bad spells, she don't like anyone."

"She drink?"

Again he was surprised. "Yeah, how'd you know?"

"That what you call an ed-u-cated guess. Person can't get long with no one, they prob'ly drink, or they on dope, or sick some kinda way." She nodded her head at Katie. "Her daddy be on dope and we can't live with him, no kinda way in the world. My momma throw him out."

Katie said, "I got my gran'daddy, right, Martha?"

"Right," Martha laughed. "You got big ears, too!"

Almost to himself, Brian said, "Well, you can't throw your mother out."

"Nope," Martha said slowly. "You jus got to get long the best way you can, till yo gets grown."

Brian felt better just telling Martha about his mother. He'd never talked to anyone about her before. He and Eve talked, but that was mainly about what to do. Go here, get that, stay out of the way.

"When she start drinking, your momma?" Martha asked. "After your daddy leave, or before?"

Brian tried to think. He squinted up his eyes and concentrated, and then he heard it in his head, a gruff, growled remark: "Aw, leave the kid alone!" That was it, that was his father, telling her not to pick on him the way she always did, for no reason.

He looked up at Martha, excited. "I remember, it was before he left! She's always been that way—you can't ever tell when she's going to holler and when she's not."

"Could be that why he left," Martha said.

Suddenly rage welled up in Brian. "Yeah, he told her to leave me alone, but he didn't do nothing about it! He just ran off, he didn't care nothing about me, just about himself. He left me with her! *I* gotta live with her, not him! The hell with him, he's just another rat! What's that they say about rats? They leave the stinking ship, huh? That's us, the stinking ship."

Katie was staring at Brian. She said, "My daddy go off, too. He leave me." Her mouth puckered for an instant, but then she went on: "I love my gran'daddy. Where yo gran'daddy, Brian?"

"I dunno."

"Brian, you listen to me," Martha interrupted; "you ain't no sinkin ship. You goin grow up, you goin be a man. And anytime you want to spit out some of that poison, you go on, spit it out. Don't keep it inside, else you be sinkin, for real, boy."

"Huh?"

"I mean the way you feel bout yo momma and yo daddy. Go ahead, you can tell me. I won't get mad at you. That first time, I think you jus be talkin sassy. I didn't know it be for real."

"I guess it's real, all right. Funny, I didn't think I could even remember my father."

23

"I 'member my daddy," Katie said.

"What you listening to us for, girl? Run long in, get washed for supper!"

"I better be going," Brian said. "See ya tomorrow."

When Martha went into the kitchen to help get supper, her mother said, "What the matter with that pore little skinny boy, he got no folks? Don't he really pay no attention in school?"

"I guess his folks ain't much good. He so busy worryin bout his momma, he ain't got no head left to listen what be goin on in the world."

Mrs. Houghton shook her head. "Don't look like he get nough to eat, even."

Brian walked home, wondering if Andy would be jabbering about him and Martha, giving his mother something else to get mad about. As he came down Rutger Street, he heard the faint squeaking of the chair. She seemed half asleep and didn't speak to him as he slipped past into the kitchen. He guessed nothing had happened yet, but he'd better find Andy and tell him to keep quiet, give him a new comic book or something.

He went up to his room, but Andy wasn't there. As he came back downstairs, his mother called: "Brian—'at you? Wh' yuh doing?" Brian stiffened. She didn't usually sound that bad in the afternoon.

"I just came home," Brian said.

"Ca' yer brother. Call Eve. Suppertime." He heard a sharp squeak from the chair as she lurched to her feet, and then the accompanying squeak from the screen door. Silence. A bump of chair into table, and the clank of a saucepan. Brian stood out of sight in the hall. She laughed. Brian was shocked. Then she stumbled to the door with a dish towel over her arm. Imitating an English maid on TV, she said, "Dinnah is serve'." She giggled and turned back into the kitchen.

Brian heard Eve start downstairs, and he went out back to look for Andy. "Listen," he said, "don't tell her nothing. Don't get her mad. She's bad already."

"Tell her what?" Andy said.

"Oh, nothing! Come on."

The three slipped into their chairs, and she thumped a plate of lukewarm canned beans down in front of each of them. Andy's sloshed onto the table, and he made a face. She turned her own chair to face the television and picked up her can of beer. They ate uneasily, glad of the TV's chatter.

Eve said, "I'm taking my plate outside. I want to watch for Henry. He's coming by for me."

"Uh-oh," Andy grinned. "Hey, you know what? Brian's got a girl friend!"

"You're kidding!" Eve paused, half smiled. Brian had never gone with any girl.

Low and intense, Brian snapped at Andy: "I told you—shut *up!*"

His tone of voice caught his mother's attention. "Sh'up y'self! Eat y' dinner!" She focused on him blearily.

Eve started to go out the screen door, and hurriedly Andy yelped, "It's fat Martha!"

"Who's she?" Eve's eyes flitted from Andy's grinning face to Brian's furious one. He was glaring down at the table now, trying to ignore Andy.

"She used to baby-sit for the Lawrences next door. Remember?"

"Oh, her. She's black."

"Sure is! And *fat!* Fat black Mar . . ." His words were drowned as Brian's chair screeched back, and he reached across the table to grab Andy by the hair. Andy yowled, a glass of Kool-Aid tipped over, and Brian yelled again, "Shut up! I'll kill you if . . ."

"Gitoutaheah!" Their mother stood up and launched herself at Brian, slapping him with her free hand.

Brian backed away, and Andy pulled free. He danced back and sang out, "Fat black Martha! Brian's sweetie!"

His mother swayed, staring at Andy, and he couldn't tell if she understood what he was saying. Her face was ugly, angry, and he began to wish he hadn't started the whole joke. She swung around toward Brian. Momentarily, her voice cleared. "I'll teach you . . ."

Expertly, Brian pushed a chair between them and slid out the door. Eve got out of his way, and he took off down the street.

He walked for a long time, not noticing where he went, not thinking anything. He wiped his mind blank, like a clean blackboard. His legs walked along, his eyes watched traffic lights, occasionally he even said, "Hi" to someone, but no pictures appeared in his mind. It was safer that way.

He stopped at a street corner on Jefferson Avenue, the big street, and realized he had focused on something. It was a dog. It had a tan face and black ears, and a tail like a wet sash. Its hindquarters trembled as it stood partly in the alley, trying to figure out how to cross the busy street.

Automatically, Brian snapped his fingers and chirped with his tongue. The black ears pricked up like signal flags. Then the dog looked behind him fearfully and set off down the sidewalk, giving up the avenue crossing. Brian followed.

The dog crossed the next little street, ignoring Brian. His whole body moved on a slight slant as he trotted. Brian noticed it and thought, How come dogs run sideways like that? It was the first definite idea that had been in his head. He concentrated on the dog, really following him now.

There was an alley running off the street, and Brian expected the dog would disappear down that. The dog paused at the corner and looked back at Brian. It was the first time he sat down. His skinny hindquarters were tucked neatly under him and his ears pricked up. He turned his head a little on a slant, as if he could watch Brian better that way.

Brian stopped. He thought, If I go any farther, he'll run down the alley, and I'll lose him. He whistled again and called, "Here, Slanty boy!"

The dog's nose stretched toward Brian a little, but he didn't move. There was a noise up the street, and the dog's eyes flicked away, then back to Brian.

Brian looked around. There was no one in sight. Slowly he sat down on the curb. He reached his hand out toward the dog, palm up, as if maybe he had some food on it, and called again. "Here, Slanty. Here, boy. Come here."

The nose stretched toward him, farther and farther, and then the front paws walked forward, until the dog was crouched. His eyes fixed on Brian, he started crawling forward, inch by inch, but as if an enormous rubber band was continually pulling him back. Brian kept on crooning, "Here, boy. Come here. Come, Slanty."

Finally the cold nose reached his fingertip. It sniffed the fingers, then the palm. Not moving his hand, Brian leaned way down. He could see all the soft tan hairs on the dog's nose, and the black whiskers, and then the dog's tongue reached out to lick his chin, then his ear. Slowly he moved his hand and scratched the dog behind the ears.

The dog sat down beside him. Brian smiled. He had the dog.

chapter
three

WHEN DWAYNE WOKE UP in the morning,
almost always the first thing he heard was that
lady yakking about the soap that got her baby's
diapers *so* white, cause she put *so* much *love* in
with them. Dwayne would stretch, shut his eyes
again, and wonder if his mother waited for that
particular commercial every morning, to wake
him. Why couldn't she get the one for wide-
track tires, or razor blades—anything but diapers?

He opened his eyes, because his mother was
back in the doorway. "Come on, boy, let me see
them feet hit the floor, fore I goes to work." She

wouldn't trust him to get up on his own, after she'd left, so Dwayne struggled out.

"Good-bye. Be a good boy." She kissed him, and Dwayne yawned his way into the bathroom. After he'd washed and dressed and combed his head thoroughly with the pic, and stuck the pic in the back of his hair, he felt human. He went into the kitchen and sniffed. Umm, biscuits. His mother had wrapped them in a paper napkin to keep warm, and he split one, buttered it carefully, and put it back together before putting it in his mouth. With his mouth full, he went to the refrigerator and poured some pineapple juice. Then he sat down. He took a bite of buttery biscuit, then a drink of the tingly, slightly sour juice. They tasted good together.

On the television, the announcer was running on with the news. Vietnam . . . the President . . . flood in Virginia . . . construction workers strike . . . Dwayne heard a black man talking and swung around to watch. A man in a hard hat, over in East St. Louis, said the construction company was hiring white guys from out of state, instead of black dudes what lived there. Dwayne chewed on his biscuit. Why they wanna do that? he thought. Sound dumb. The picture flickered on to a lady talking about some meeting. When the little kiddie show came on, he knew it was time to leave for school.

He finished his breakfast and took his plate to the sink. He could just hear his mother's voice saying, "Nothin get me so mad as to come in here and find flies buzzin round ole breakfast dishes!"

He picked up his lunch bag and peered inside —more biscuits, ham, pickle, cookies. He tucked it under his arm, glanced around the kitchen to see if it was tidy, flipped off the TV, and went out.

It was quiet and cool out. The little kids next door weren't even fighting each other yet. Dwayne got to his friend Terry's house and whistled. He could hear Terry's mother from out on the sidewalk. She was nagging as usual.

Terry came out the door, and then she really hollered at him. He'd forgotten his lunch.

"Man, you really off to a good start, this day!" Dwayne said.

"I wish she was workin, like yo momma," Terry sighed. "Then I just stay home all day, enjoy myself."

"My old man come home and bust my butt, if I stay home," Dwayne said.

"Lucky my old man ain't home, my momma is bout all I can stand!"

They got to the schoolyard and Dwayne went over to the girls' line to find Melvita.

They chattered together until the teacher's voice rang out: "Dwayne, are you one of the girls this morning?"

"No, ma'am, me and Melvita be on this committee. We got to report on an ex-spear-ment . . ."

"Get over where you belong!" she hollered.

"Yes, ma'am," Dwayne sighed. He ambled

31

away as if his feet were weighted, snapping his fingers slowly and letting his midsection move with a life of its own.

In the boys' line, Brian seemed to be looking straight through him. That boy, he thought, just don't see. He don't even know he looked right at me the other day, down to Soulard. So Dwayne walked right past him, as close as he could come without bumping, but Brian never blinked.

Up in the classroom, Mr. Cousins put morning work on the blackboard out of habit. A few minutes later, when he stepped out of the room, Dwayne slid in beside Melvita.

"What we goin do all summer? We got to think," he said.

"I don't got to think nothin at all. I baby-sit Precious Coleman, that what."

"You sick of that spoiled kid already. Why don't you get something else?"

"Cause her momma pay me good, that why!" Melvita jabbed him with her elbow. "Quit squeezin! This desk too small for two people in June!"

"All you care about is money! All right, I's goin. And when I make me a pile of money you won't see me at all!"

"Huh! I see you soon enough! Next time you need to borrow a buck—you'll be there!" Melvita imitated the popular song.

Dwayne walked away. Money was a sore point between them, because she usually had it, and he usually didn't.

A little way down the row, Dwayne sat in front of two girls who were playing checkers. He rested his chin on the chair back. "Little girl, if I was you, I move me that man and get me a king," he said.

"You ain't me, and get your cotton-pickin hands off!"

"Ain't no cotton picker! I's one hip cat!"

She giggled. "I see you eatin that corn bread and beans for your lunch!"

The boy next to her said, "He buy his shoes in the hardware store for a dollar sixty-nine. Them ones with the big square toes!"

"They for kickin you with, boy," Dwayne grinned.

There was a sudden hush in the classroom. "Dwayne, why are you out of your coat?" Mr. Cousins was back.

"Suh, I be huntin for my old green pencil, the one with the little bitty eraser. I can't do my mornin work . . ."

Kids laughed, and the teacher stared at him until he wandered back to his own desk and collapsed into it with a disconsolate thud. The day went on. In the back of his head, Dwayne kept wondering, What can I do all summer? Got to get me some money, so that Melvita don't act like she Miss Moneybags.

After school, Terry and some other boys wanted him to play ball, but he didn't feel like it. He waited for Melvita. But when she came out, she didn't even look over at him. She went by in a group of girls cackling like chickens. He could pick her out of the bunch, her head bobbing along a little taller than the others, her big legs swinging. "Cause she got big legs, big mouth, big money, she think she so baad," Dwayne muttered.

He didn't feel like going home, so he walked the other way, south, toward where they were building the new Interstate. He found a place in the shade to sit and watched the huge machines rumbling past, churning up the dust. One came fairly close, and the tires on it were the size of a whole ordinary car. That'd be good, driving one of them, Dwayne thought.

He looked up at the drivers. They had on hard hats, dust caked their faces like a mask, and their eyes bored straight ahead, to see where they were driving. Dwayne remembered that black man talking on TV in the morning. He looked again at the drivers. Their faces were dirty, all right, but they were white.

Restless, dissatisfied, Dwayne left his shady spot and walked along in the dust, until he came to Mississippi Avenue, where traffic could cross the construction. He looked at the man in a hard hat there, too, directing traffic. His face was dusty like the others, sweaty, tired looking. Black.

He looked at Dwayne, and faint smile lines creased the dust on his face. "Hey, boy!" he said.

"Hey, Pop," Dwayne answered and walked on. Man, he thought, that ain't no kind of job to have. Other cats kick up the dust, and he stand there and breathe it.

The dust made him thirsty, and he wished now he'd gone home, but he went on walking south. Unconsciously, he walked more warily. Southside—he could just hear his father's voice, warning him, stay outta there, boy.

He remembered the night they heard that his cousin Leo had got arrested. Leo had just been walking home from the movies, cutting through Longfellow, that quiet street with the big houses, when the cops picked him up and said he mugged some lady, and Leo said he didn't, but he had money on him. He just got paid that day.

Dwayne remembered his father finishing the story, a year later. "So they turn Leo loose today; they can't prove nothin gainst him. So they don't care how long they lock him up—he lose his job, lose his car—now he probably go out and mug somebody for real!" And he turned to Dwayne. "You stay outta that Southside, boy —ain't no place for you!"

Glancing around him as he walked, Dwayne saw that there were only white people around him on the street. He walked carefully, not bumping into anyone, trying not to catch anyone's eye. Still, if he did catch someone's eye, he wouldn't drop his own. He stared glassily.

He hunted for stores, a small grocery or drugstore that might need a delivery boy. He came to one called the Missouri Superette. A lady was trying to push her way out the door, holding a big bag of groceries in one hand and her little girl's hand with the other. Dwayne held the door for her, and then he thought, Maybe I carry her groceries home, I get enough for a soda.

"Carry your groceries, ma'am?" he said.

Dwayne noticed that when she looked at him her face tightened up. She snapped, "I can manage!" She grabbed her groceries and her little girl and hurried away from him. It was like a slap in the face. Dwayne stared after her. Then he plunged into the store.

Behind the counter, a freckle-faced redhead was making change for customers. Somehow, Dwayne knew before he asked that it was hopeless, but he had to ask anyway.

"You the manager?" he said, and his voice came out sounding defiant.

"I guess so."

"Uh, you need a delivery boy, stock boy, for the summer?"

"How old are you, boy?"

"Fifteen," he said, which wasn't quite true.

The man started checking groceries for the next customer. "Sorry, I can't hire anyone under sixteen."

Dwayne turned and went back onto the hot sunny street. He headed for home, walking fast with his head down, not looking at anyone. He thought, He wouldn't hire me even if I was sixteen. He was sure the man, the store, the streets, the whole place were against him.

He crossed the Interstate and was glad to be back in his own territory. When he got home, his mother was standing at the stove and his father was reading the paper, his shoes and shirt off. He looked up. "Where you been at, boy?"

"Daddy, I got to get me a job this summer. What can I do?"

"Porch need painting," his father said. He owned the house and was proud of that. It was the first house in St. Louis they'd owned.

"That ain't no job!"

"It need doing, it be a job, all right."

"Aw, you know what I mean—I got to get a job where they be paying me."

"You do a good job, I might pay you some for painting."

"I could do that porch in a coupla days—that ain't nothin."

His mother said, "Yo daddy be makin good money, nough for all of us. Your main job bes to get an *education*, that what you got to do. And help your daddy round home. Time enough later for jobs."

"Momma, you don't understand! I need a job *now!*"

"Why for?"

"Cause I jus do. Anybody know that." Dwayne lapsed into sulky silence, and his father went on reading, and his mother mashed the potatoes.

They ate dinner, and it was good, but still Dwayne couldn't shake his grouch. He hardly listened to his parents' routine conversation; it had nothing to do with the way he felt. Trapped. Anywhere he went, nothing to do. No work, nothing happening at school. No one to talk to. He finished his dinner and pushed back his chair.

His father looked at him. "Boy, you leave the table, you say 'Excuse me' to your momma!"

"Scuse me," Dwayne mumbled, but to himself, He picking on me all the time. Treat me like a baby.

He pushed out the door into the street. "Don't be late, Dwayne!" his mother called after him. He scuffed down the block, kicking stones and bits of broken glass. Late, he snorted. Where would I go, late? Ain't no place to go no way. Down to Happy Jack's, same like always.

Happy Jack's was a candy store out on Eighteenth Avenue. Happy kept his door locked and the windows had long since been boarded up, but there was a little window where you could say what you wanted, soda or candy or chips, and put your money down. Happy kept the radio near the opening, so the music poured out into the street. He liked having the kids around. When they went home, he closed up the little window and went upstairs, where he lived.

Dwayne shoved his hands into his pockets and then stopped, stood still in the street. No money. Not even a dime for candy at Happy's. Go home and ask Dad? He scowled. Lend it off Melvita? He scowled again. Ain't goin around with a poor mouth. Do without, what's the difference? He continued down the block, saw an empty soda bottle in the gutter. It was still in one piece, and he kicked it. It broke and Dwayne muttered, Good! Ain't no use in two cents anyway.

He got to Happy's and hung around the edge of the group. Melvita wasn't there anyway. Her friends were—Corita, Sharon, Geniann—but she didn't feel like fooling with them. Terry and big

Jasper were standing together, eating chips and soda. They had money.

Dwayne moved down to the corner. A bunch of bigger kids were standing around, not eating or joking, but listening to one big cat. Dwayne knew him—his name was James. He was one of the kids at McKinley High School, and he was always making speeches and trying to get the kids to do something. Now he was trying to get them to go on strike. James didn't like the dude who was teaching Black Studies, because he was a fussy old historian who didn't know anything about Black.

Dwayne listened with one ear. School was just fooling around or some days just boring. Nothing to make speeches about anyway. The only thing he could be serious about was getting a job and getting some money. He wanted Melvita to be his girl, really, and he wanted to have money to spend when he was with her. It wasn't that she nagged him to spend money. It was just that he wanted to know himself that he had it.

"Man, I wish I was in high school!" Dwayne looked around. It was fat Martha, by herself, and talking to herself or the world. For once she wasn't eating anything, and Dwayne was glad to lean against the fence with her and talk.

"What we all got to go through eighth grade for?" Martha went on. "They ain't goin to teach us nothin new."

"Same ole, same ole," Dwayne agreed.

"Mr. Cousins, he the only good teacher, and he leavin."

"How come he leavin?"

"He say he sick and tired of bustin up fights in the yard."

Dwayne laughed. "We have us some good fights out there. Only good thing in school, cept sports." He rocked lightly on the balls of his feet and shadowboxed.

"Why you cats got to fight all the time? Don't do no good."

"You don't fight, you don't get nothin," Dwayne said. "You's a chicken."

"But you jus fightin with each other—you still ain't gettin nothin. Lookit now, we lose the only good teacher we got."

"Ain't my fault. Probably get hisself a better job, someplace else. Who want to hang round Clinton?"

"Yeah. Who want to hang round here, either? I'm goin." Martha nodded and walked off. Dwayne looked once more at the kids around the candy store, but Melvita still wasn't there. He walked slowly home.

chapter
four

By Friday, Dwayne had shaken off his
blues. He'd pitched a winning baseball game,
earned fifty cents cleaning up a yard, and there
was a teachers' meeting, so the day was free.
Melvita said she didn't have to work, so after
breakfast he headed for her house, which was on
a little street called Vail Place, in back of the
park.

He went through the alley and approached
the house warily. Melvita's mother see me
comin, he thought, she find something Melvita
got to do.

Melvita's baby brother ran out of the house

EMILY CHENEY NEVILLE

laughing, with no pants on. Melvita was right
behind him and scooped him up. Dwayne whistled.

Melvita waited for him. "Momma ain't up yet
—I got to watch the kids. Here, hold him a minute."

"He ain't got no pants on—he might do it all
over me!"

"Dumdum, he already did it, that why he got
'em off!" Melvita went in the house and came
back with the baby's pants and some toys. She
sat down on the step beside Dwayne.

"How long you got to baby-sit?" he asked.

"What time it is?"

"Almost ten o'clock."

Melvita thought for a minute, and then stood
up. "She could wake up now. You wait for me,
down by the alley—I tell her I go to the store.
Remember to stop me at the store fore I come
home, so she can't say I tell a lie!"

When she joined him, she said, "What we goin
to do?"

"I got fifty cents. You want to go up to Forest
Park?"

"We got to get us some rides. I got to be back
by four o'clock. Got to go to Mrs. Coleman—she
be workin evenins now."

"You mean you got to work in the evenin
now? Man, that's a dumb job! Why don't you
quit?"

"I quit, I be workin at home, and I don't even
get paid nothin for that."

"How much that Mrs. Coleman pay you, huh?"

42

"None of your business, boy!"

"You love that money so, you make me sick! Whatcha gonna do with it all?"

"Goin to get my own house someday, and it gonna be all clean and new! Ain't goin to be no kids makin wet beds, no cockroaches jumpin outta beer cans!"

"You can't get your own house—you jus a kid!"

"Well, anything you want, you got to have money. Without money, you is nothin!"

Dwayne didn't like hearing that, since he'd been thinking it himself for days.

"Come on, girl, get yo mind off yo money! I race you to the corner!"

They saw a boy they knew driving toward the park and got a ride. They walked in by the zoo, and Dwayne bought a box of popcorn. Melvita said, "Now—what we goin to do? I been in that zoo more than enough times."

"We could go swim in the fountain, down the bottom of the hill."

"You crazy! I ain't goin to swim in my clothes! Sides, cops throw you out."

"They don't throw those white kids out."

"Ahh—they rich."

"Rich! Girl, you crazy! Lookit those dirty old clothes they wearin."

"They still rich—they daddies be sendin them to college, don't they? So they got money."

"If I had me a lot of money, I get me some gators and some silk shirts, and I be learnin how

43

to drive one of them great big ole road machines. You get a lot of money drivin big machines like that."

"You don't wear no silk shirts and gators drivin a bulldozer."

"Ain't no bulldozer, girl. Ten times that big—a regular elephandozer. And I wear my baad clothes time I go dancin with my chick."

"Well, what I want to know—where you takin this here chick right now?"

They had been walking along, and Dwayne looked up and saw a big building ahead of them, with a glass roof. Might be a basketball court, Dwayne thought.

"I takin you in there, girl. Come along, pick up them big feet!"

Melvita giggled. "Oooweee, look it say 'Jewel Box.' That be great—I love to look at jewels!"

"A-w-w—I was thinkin we might see a basketball game! Who need jewels?"

"I do."

Dwayne saw a turnstile at the door. "Uh-oh, you got to pay."

"So—you the big spender. Come on!"

"Yeah, but look—it need a quarter for each of us, and I done spent a dime on popcorn."

"You dumdum, what you have to go buy that old popcorn for?" Melvita said, ignoring the fact that she'd eaten half of it. "So now what we going to do? You ain't interested anyway. You going to pay for me to go look at the jewels, right?"

"You think I'm goin to stand out here waitin

for you, lookin like a lamppost? You got another thought comin!"

Melvita turned around and nibbled the end of one finger, concentrating. Down by the fountains, she saw two ladies in fresh pretty dresses, carrying big shiny pocketbooks.

She grabbed Dwayne by the sleeve and pulled him along. "Scuse me, ma'am," she said to the ladies. "I surely hate to trouble you. Our teacher send us up here to the Jewel Box, to make a report for our committee, and she don't tell us you got to pay a quarter. She surely going to be disappointed, we don't make no report."

"Don't make *any* report, dear," one lady said.

"Yes, ma'am."

"What school do you go to?" the other lady asked.

"Clinton School, ma'am."

"And what is your committee reporting on?"

"Ah-h—precious jewels."

The two ladies laughed and looked at each other. One said, "I'm afraid you may be disappointed, dear."

The other said, "Are you sure she sent you here to look at precious jewels?"

"Yes, ma'am." Melvita couldn't see what had gone wrong.

Dwayne said, "See, ma'am, we got to report on all kind of precious things. Don't matter what kind. Our teacher don't mind what we look at, long as it be precious."

The ladies laughed again, and one opened her pocketbook and gave them each a quarter.

"Thank you, ma'am!" Dwayne said.

"We surely do preciate your kindness," Melvita got off before they turned and ran toward the Jewel Box, laughing together when they were out of earshot.

Inside the building, Dwayne and Melvita suddenly stopped short. It was the smell they noticed first, a wonderful warm, wet, sweet smell. The air was different, and there in front of them was a whole different world. The building was filled with trees and plants and flowers, planted along little curving walks. It was a magic world, and they were right in it. The Jewel Box was a house of flowers.

"O-o-o!" Melvita let out a long sigh. They looked, and after a bit she said, "There be a little house to live in, even. See, that what I want, a little house just like that!"

Dwayne was impressed too. "It got a waterfall in it. You think anybody live here?"

"I dunno. Dwayne, how about if we could live here? We might go to school and places, daytimes. Then we come back here at night and we have the whole place to ourselves. How bout that?"

"Mmmm." Dwayne breathed in deeply.

"We can walk around," Melvita said. They walked along the paths, sometimes slowly, sometimes running, looking at different plants and the signs on them. They came to a fountain, and the bottom of it was covered with pennies.

Dwayne took out a nickel, shut his eyes tight

a moment, and flicked it in. "What you wish?" Melvita said.

"Can't say. You say, and it don't come true."

They were interrupted by a laugh. "My! A whole nickel! Isn't that a lot for a wish?" It was the two ladies who had given them money.

Dwayne straightened up, and his black eyes shone. "Ma'am, my wish is worth a whole lot more than a nickel! And I goin to have me a whole lot of nickels someday! Come on, Melvita!"

They walked away, while the two ladies stood and stared. "Well!" said one.

"My!" said the other.

"Do you suppose—they had money all along?" The ladies shook their heads.

Melvita and Dwayne ran out of the Jewel Box and raced each other, one on each side of the fountains and gardens. They got to the far end, panting and laughing.

"Sure be one pretty place," Melvita said. "We got to come back here."

"What I want, be to live there."

"Mmm. It smell so good. Think of all that good smell wasted at night, no one there."

"Maybe we could hide in that little house at closin time."

"They find you."

"Yeah." They walked along in the sun. Dwayne said, "Dusty out here. A soda would go good."

"Ain't you the big-time spender! Popcorn, wishing well—come on, boy, tell me. What you wish?" Melvita hung on his arm.

Dwayne swaggered his shoulders. "It come true, you find out!"

"You mean I'm in your wish?"

"Don't go puttin words in my mouth for me. Come on, we gettin a soda!"

They bought a soda and split it and walked back into the park to the side where there were plenty of trees and bushes for shade. Couples were sprawled here and there on the grass, on blankets, under blankets.

Melvita giggled. "They play house."

"Don't stare, it ain't nice!" Dwayne put his arm around her shoulders and steered her toward a thick yew bush. "Here, Mister Park Commissioner grow this house just for you and me!"

They wiggled in under the bush, hidden from view, where they could whisper and lie together in their own house.

After a long time, Melvita sat up. "I got to get home, time to go to work."

Dwayne snorted. "That all you can think of!"

She tried to be soothing. "It ain't all, but still I got to get there. We can't live here, any more than in that Jewel Box. Now, how we goin to get home?"

Dwayne scowled. There was exactly one dime and one penny in his pocket. "We got to get us a ride again."

"We don't know no one round here."

"We hitchhike."

"Oooo . . ." Melvita frowned. Slowly she opened her own little pocketbook and took out the change purse. "I got a little money. Les see, fifty, sixty cents, coupla three four pennies. Ain't enough for *two* bus fares."

"So." Dwayne stood up. "Like I tell you, we hitchhike."

"Dwayne, my momma kill me, she find out I hitchhike. Sides, I'm scared. Maybe I better catch me a bus."

Dwayne flared up. "That the way you feel, is it? Jus go off, take a bus by yo own self, don't care nothin bout me!"

"Dwayne, I'm sorry, honest I is! But I got to get to my job."

"Job! Money! All you think about! You ain't my chick, yo just an ole moneybags! Any dude got money, you . . ."

"Better watch yo mouth, boy!" Melvita yelled. She jumped up and faced him, hands on hips, her chin out.

"Aww . . ." Dwayne shifted his eyes and scuffed his feet. "You goin take yoself home, you goin do it. Go head. Don't matter none to me."

"Dwayne, honey, listen . . ."

"Listen to what?"

"I don't want to leave. I want to stay, but . . ."

"But!" he mimicked.

"Ain't there no way we can get us two bus fares?"

"Hey, wait. I got an idea!" He dropped on his knees and started crawling slowly over the grass.

"Boy, have you gone clean outta yo mind? Dogs don't find no money and sides I hate dogs! Get up!"

"Unh-unh." He shook his head. "C'mon, get

down here and help me look. See, one other day I seen a dude with one of them metal detector things. Look like a vacuum cleaner. So I say, 'Man, you trying to clean up this park?' And he say, 'Yeah, I clean up five, ten dollars somedays.' See this park been here bout a hundred years. Lotta people been droppin their money all that time. Specially them dudes, rollin round on the grass with they girl friend." Dwayne laughed, then pounced in the grass. "See! I got a dime! C'mon, girl, get to lookin!"

Melvita found a nickel. Then they put all their money together, including the pennies, and they were one penny short of two bus fares.

"Maybe the bus man let us get on. Come on, I got to go," Melvita said.

Dwayne walked over to a kid in blue jeans who was sitting with his girl. "Hey, mister, would you lend me a penny?"

"Sure, I guess. When you going to pay me back?"

"First of the month," Dwayne said. "You be here, see."

"I'll be here," the kid said.

"Right on. See, I don't b'lieve in borrowing. That ain't too cool!" Dwayne went back to Melvita and they set off for the bus stop, running.

They reached Vail Place and Melvita hurried along. "Wait up out here, Dwayne, see if she holler at me."

Dwayne hung back a little and waited and sure enough, pretty soon he heard an angry voice, a slap, and Melvita crying. Dwayne cocked his head and listened. She ain't crying for real, he thought, that just to satisfy her momma.

In a few minutes, Melvita came out, dragging a laundry cart. There weren't any tears on her face, but she sniffled, "She make me do the laundry, and I goin to be late for work! That Mrs. Coleman can't be late—she got to be at the hospital on time. What I'm goin to do?" She sniffed again and looked at Dwayne.

Dwayne knew real crying from get-something crying. He whistled up at a bird in the tree and said, "What was you thinking of doin?"

Melvita giggled. "Dwayne, honey, please! We go and I get the clothes all in the machines and do the soap and stuff, and you could just take them out, huh? Please, Dwayne?"

"How long that take?"

"Well, they got to go in the dryer."

Dwayne smacked his forehead. "Girl, you givin me an hour's work! What you payin me?"

"Listen, I pay yo bus fare already, most of it."

"Huh! That yo idea, not mine!"

"So what I got to pay you?"

"Mmm, I settle for a soda and a bag of chips."

Melvita groaned. "All right! Here I thought you my friend, thought you goin to do me a favor."

"I thought you got so much money you don't need to ask no favors from nobody."

"Well, I jus like you, so I like for you to do me favors!"

"Mmm—sweet talk!" They turned into the

Laundromat and Melvita got the wash started, and he said, "O.K., girl, you can go to that precious job!"

"Dwayne, I love you!"

"Tell me that someday you don't want nothin!"

He watched her go, then picked up the beat from a radio that was playing and bopped over to the soda machine. He circled the Laundromat for a while, then fished an old comic out of the basket and looked at it. He put the clothes into the dryer, watched them tumble and shadow-boxed with them. A white-haired old lady at the next machine laughed. "You going to be Muhammad Ali the second, is you, boy?"

"Yes, ma'am!"

"You good boy, you be helpin your mother, right?"

"No, ma'am, I workin for my girl friend today!"

The old lady laughed as if he'd said something really funny. When the clothes finished tumbling, he piled them into the laundry cart. He cocked his head and held up a little pair of black bikini underpants and winked at the old lady, and she laughed some more. He sashayed out of the Laundromat pulling the cart.

Outside, he ran into Terry and some of the boys coming home with their baseball mitts and ball. "Hey, Sisi, your momma sure be workin you hard today!" Terry jeered.

Dwayne scowled. It'd be worse if he told them he was doing Melvita's laundry. "I do the laundry when I feel like it. Too hot for baseball." That was the best he could manage, and he waited till they were out of sight before turning toward Melvita's. In front of the others, he wanted to be the one going to the job, and Melvita the one doing the laundry.

chapter
five

BRIAN FOUND SLANTY on the same block
every night that week. He brought him food, he
tried to get the dog to follow him home, but
Slanty wouldn't come along. Finally, Brian
brought the end of a hot dog. "You're going to
be my friend, right, Slanty? You stay with me.
I'll buy you things. You like pretzels, huh,
Slanty?"

The dog wriggled its behind on the sidewalk
and licked quickly at his mouth.

"I haven't got any money right now, Slanty,
but I'll get some. You want to come home with
me? You want to sleep on my bed?"

Loud voices and a clatter of shoes came around the corner. Instantly the dog slipped across the street into the shadows. Brian crossed, too, away from the noisy kids approaching. The dog skittered on ahead of him down to the next corner. When the kids had gone, the dog let Brian catch up with him. They walked along, not quite together, but going the same way. When they reached Brian's house, Brian turned in, and the dog sat abruptly, ears cocked, head aslant, curious.

There was no one sitting on the porch and no noise from the kitchen, not even the television going. Brian said, "Here, Slanty. Come on, boy. I live here."

The dog lay down, its nose on its front paws, pointing at Brian, eyes wide open. Brian came back and petted him, then moved toward the house again, coaxing. "Come on, Slanty." But Slanty lay there.

Brian ran up the steps and into the kitchen. He stood there a moment listening. No sound. They must have all gone to bed. It must be late. Quietly, he opened a cupboard and found two pieces of bread. He went back to Slanty and broke off a little piece for him. Then he moved toward the house, holding out more bread, and Slanty followed.

On the porch, Brian sat down and patted the space beside him on the long, rickety, swinging couch. The dog jumped up. Brian fed him pieces of bread and ate some himself. He lay down on the couch and Slanty curled himself into the corner made by his knees, as if he'd always slept there. When Brian's mother stumbled up the steps late that night, the dog raised its head.

Martha woke up and yawned happily, knowing before she opened her eyes that it was Saturday. She didn't have to hurry. When she opened them, she saw that her sister's bed was empty. More luxury, the room all to herself.

She picked up her book from the floor and read for a while. Then she got up and tidied things on her bureau. She turned and caught sight of herself in the long mirror. The day went sour.

Usually when she got up, she went straight into the bathroom, washed, and fixed her hair in front of the little round mirror there. She combed it out into a big fluffy cloud, and her face looked round and pretty under the cloud. She could imagine a graceful, slim body below.

Now she was looking at the real thing. Her stomach and hips bulged against the thin nightgown. Its sprigged roses looked stretched and ugly. Her arms hung out of the sleeveless gown like big brown rolls. She hated herself. She thought, Anyone look at me, they be disgusted. Then they tell a joke and laugh, pretend they ain't disgusted.

Her mouth tightened in a thin miserable line, the only thin thing about her. She looked at her fat and thought about food, and that made her even more miserable. I got to stop eatin, she thought. Nothing for breakfast. No sweet rolls. No ham and eggs. No hot chocolate. After school, no doughnuts, no ice cream, no pizzas. Miserably she turned away from the mirror. How could you face a whole day with no food to think about? What good was Saturday, or any other day?

She dressed and came downstairs, attacked by all the good smells from the kitchen. She mumbled good morning and grabbed a diet soda to take out on the porch. In a little while her mother came out.

"You feelin bad, girl?"

"No."

"How come you not eatin?"

Words suddenly came out in a rush. "Ma, I just can't stand being fat, fat, FAT all the time! I just wanta die!" Martha started crying.

"Now, honey, you just take it easy. Maybe this hot weather make you feel miserable. Lots of girls be heavy when they young. You be skinny as a stringbean, after you get married."

"Married! No one gonna marry a fat hog like me!"

"Shush, now jus hush! You got more friends than anyone."

"Yeah, 'cause I'm a big joke they all can laugh at! Fat Martha, ha, ha, ha!"

"Come on, let me fix you a little bitty breakfast. Just some juice and a soft-boiled egg, that won't fatten . . ."

"Momma, you know I can't eat a little! I eat at all, I be eatin the whole thing! Jus like a pig. No, ma'am, I ain't eatin no breakfast!" She heaved

herself out of the chair and walked out to the
street, and across to the park.

Her mother shook her head and smoothed her
apron across her own thin stomach. She couldn't
stand to see children unhappy, and the easiest
way she knew to make children happy was to
cook up good food.

Martha scuffed along the sidewalk to the far
side of the park. She paused and looked up at
the treetops. The sun was just hitting them and
the leaves wiggled in the soft breeze. Martha
sniffed and thought, Air be like people, fresh in
the mornin, all dragged out by evenin. Only air
don't get hungry. . . .

She walked down to the pond and looked over
the still water. A fisherman moved slowly, to
throw his line out. She looked past him and
stopped. "That Brian!" she said out loud. That
crazy boy, what he doin sittin in the park all by
himself on a Saturday mornin? She started
around the pond toward him. When she got
closer, she saw he was reaching into a box and
munching on dry cereal.

"Boy, what you doin, eatin dry shred wheat?
Ain't no good that way—it need milk and sugar!"

"Uh—it's not for me. I brought it for my dog."

"What dog? I don't see no dog."

"Well, I just got him."

"So where he at? I surely don't see him. All I
see is you munchin on dry cereal." With a will of
its own, her hand reached out, dug into the box,
and came out with a handful for her to nibble.
"Where this dog at, huh?"

"I lost him."

"You jus get him and you lose him already?"

"Well, see, he was a stray dog. I found him up on Jefferson, and after a while he let me pet him. So every night this week, I've been with him, but last night he followed me home, and I fed him, and ..."

"And what? He run off again, right?"

"N-no. We were sitting on the porch, and then I lay on the couch and the dog jumped up with me, and we fell asleep, I guess. And I guess my mom came home, and I don't know what happened. I was on the floor, and she was kicking me, and then the dog yelped. You know, like he was really hurt. And he ran away."

"Your momma kick you or the dog?"

"Both. She don't know what she was doing ..."

"She drunk, huh?"

"Yeah."

"So what happen to you?"

"Well, I heard the dog yipping down the street, and she was yelling at me, and I just ran inside and up to my room. She didn't come up after me. She slept on the couch all night. She's still there."

"Boy, you sure got trouble. Where yo sister at?"

"Home. I didn't see her this morning."

"So now what you doin—huntin for that little ole dog, to take him home, to make yo momma mad all over again?"

Brian's mouth closed stubbornly and he didn't answer. Martha said, "Huh?"

"Well, I got to find him, at least. I want to see if he's O.K. He must of been really scared. He didn't go back where I used to find him. And I got to feed him, too. He was awful hungry."

Martha's hand reached out to the box again. "Know what, this stuff ain't so bad after all. Good idea, eating it without milk and sugar— you just can't eat too much of it. Can't hardly get it down!" She laughed suddenly.

"What's so funny?"

"I ain't laughin at you—I just laughin at us sittin here in the park on a Saturday morning, munchin on dry cereal! Strike me funny, it sure do!"

"Well, it ain't finding the dog. Slanty, that's what I call him. We got to save the rest of this cereal for him."

"O.K., come on—I help you hunt. Where you look already?"

"All around the park. Up on Jefferson."

"You ask anyone?"

"Unh-unh."

"That's what you gotta do, boy—you got to ask people. Somebody seen him, you can be sure of that."

Martha set off toward the corner grocery store. They went in, and Brian stood back, looking around the store. As long as there was talking to be done, he left it up to Martha. She got the storekeeper to give her a piece of paper, and she put up a sign, saying Lost Dog.

"What your address, boy?" she asked.

"Eighteen twenty-six Rutger."

"O.K., come on—we got to go to the other stores."

Outside, Brian said, "I never talked to the man in that store. He talks funny."

"He a foreigner. Greek, Polish, somethin like that. He a nice man though—he sell you candy and stuff. He don't holler at you."

They walked along the park and paused where a young woman was digging in her garden. She had on blue jeans, and her long blonde hair hung down into the dirt.

"Scuse me, ma'am," Martha said. "You see a little slanty-wise stray dog round here? Brown with black ears?"

The woman tossed her long hair back over her shoulder and wiped her face on her shirt sleeve. She laughed. "I don't see any dog's ears—all I see is their hind legs! Every one of them goes by turns up on my bushes!"

"Yes, ma'am, that surely be hard on the bushes," Martha said. She put up Lost Dog signs for him in two other stores, and then she said she had to go home. "You come round and tell me if you find him, you hear?"

"Yeah. O.K."

"Hey, Brian . . ." He stopped. ". . . You come tell me what happen with your momma, too."

"Nothing going to happen, I guess."

"Sometimes they has to take 'em to the hospital, when they be real drunk like that. They sober up in the hospital, and then they be better. For a while, anyway."

"Oh."

"You ask your sister. Maybe she know."

"She don't know."

"Boy, you got to talk to her anyway! Maybe she need you to help some. How about cousins? Ain't you got an auntie, or a gran'momma— someone would help you?"

Brian shook his head. "They stay away from us. I don't think we got any cousins that live around here anyway." He stopped, then said vaguely, "Well, I'll see you."

She looked after him and shook her head. That boy don't know about nothin. She was so used to her own relatives piling in and out on each other in times of trouble that she couldn't imagine what it would be like to be without cousins.

chapter
six

BRIAN GOT HOME, and Eve was sitting out on the side porch in the metal chair, but not bouncing and squeaking it. She had her hair in rollers, drying it in the sun, and filing her nails.

"You going someplace?" Brian asked.

"Nope. Why should I be going someplace, just because I get cleaned up?"

"I just asked."

"Well, where have you been anyway? You're always late on school days, how come you get up so early Saturday?"

"Uh—I had to hunt for my dog."

"What dog?"

"This dog I found. But he ran away again. Mom kicked him last night, when she came home dr . . ."

"Yeah, she was still asleep out here when I got up."

"Where is she now?" Brian asked softly.

Eve bobbed her head back toward the kitchen. "She had a cup of coffee in front of her when I got up, but she wasn't drinking it. Then she got a beer, and she went back to sleep. On the table."

"Can I get something to eat?"

"If you can find anything. Andy was griping that there wasn't any cereal."

"Oh, yeah, I . . ." Brian stopped, reconsidered. "What if she wakes up?"

"She won't." Eve's mouth snapped shut, but Brian looked at her and she added, "She's really passed out, she really is."

Brian edged quietly into the kitchen and sidled past his mother, not looking down at her directly. Out of the corner of his eye, he saw that her head on the table was turned away from him. He opened the refrigerator. No milk. He eased the door shut, afraid still that at some sudden noise she would jump at him. He found bread and peanut butter. He mixed instant coffee and sugar and the end of a can of milk and filled the glass with water and took it all back outside.

He ate the sandwich and drained the glass down to the sticky unmelted sugar at the bottom. It tasted pretty good, and he sucked at the last bits of peanut butter stuck to his teeth. "There's nothing much left to eat," he said to Eve.

"I know. Why don't you go to the store?"

"You got money?"

"Her City check came yesterday. She must have cashed it. Look in her pocketbook."

Brian licked at his teeth and fidgeted. "Uh . . ."

"Oh, for heavens sake!" Eve slapped down her magazine and nail file and pushed into the kitchen, letting the screen door slam. Brian heard a thick, wordless mumble from his mother, and he froze, but in a moment Eve came back out with a ten-dollar bill. "Here!" she said, and he stuffed it in his pocket. "Wait. I better make a list. You'll have to get cheap stuff—she didn't get the food stamps."

Eve thought and scribbled for a minute and passed him the list. "If you don't have enough money, leave out the peaches. Well, get a couple. I'm so sick of spaghetti I could die."

Brian looked at the list. "Do I get that spaghetti stuff in the can with sauce?"

"Get the box, it's cheaper. We're going to run out of money before the end of the month anyway."

"Can't we get the food stamps next week?"

Eve shrugged. "She quits buying food stamps when she's buying a lot of beer. She doesn't want to give them all that money for food."

Brian put the list and the money in his pocket,

then hesitated. "Eve—doesn't the City send someone around? You know, to see what she's doing with the money?"

"Yeah, but not very often. A social worker comes a few times a year. You know that."

"What if she comes when Mom's like that?" He nodded toward the kitchen.

"She won't. She came a few weeks ago. I think Mom sort of knows. Maybe people on the block tell each other when the social worker's around."

"Listen, Eve, how about— I mean, do we have any relatives? An aunt or a grandmother or something? Do they ever come?"

"Mom's mother is up in Chicago. She's old and sick. There was a sister of Daddy's who came to see us once from Illinois. It was before Daddy left, but Mom picked a fight with her, and she went away." Eve paused. She could see the whole scene in her head again, the woman running out to her car angry. Eve said, "I was just a kid, but I remember her. She had on a pretty dress, and she had on some perfume . . ."

Brian sniffed. What did it matter how they smelled? They weren't around. "So there isn't anyone who'd help us, if . . . I mean, if Mom . . ."

Eve's mouth tightened. "No, there isn't. But she'll get better. She always does. There's just a few bad days."

"I'll go get the food," Brian said.

When he came back with the groceries, he slid the bag quietly onto the table, as far from his mother as possible. Then he faded off to his room.

Eve moved around the kitchen with the normal clatter, pulling open cupboard doors and thumping packages down. She paid no more attention to her mother than if she had been an old coat on the chair. Sometimes she tried to pretend her mother was just a problem, like in algebra. You could try to work it out, or you could skip it and bluff the next class. Underneath, she knew it wasn't that kind of a problem at all. It lived with her. What if they did run out of money? Who do you go to? What if . . .? You heard about people drinking themselves to death. What if she really did it?

Eve stopped clattering and stood very still to listen. Her mother's breath came in wheezes and her back rose and fell. She was alive, all right. But would she always get over it, with just a few bad days? Eve sighed, finished with the groceries, and grabbed one of the three peaches from a little bag. She sunk her teeth into the ripe pink side and the juice spurted. What a relief, after all that dead-white spaghetti!

Brian settled on the edge of his bed and flipped the pages of a comic, but he didn't really see the pictures. He saw his mother asleep on the table, and he heard the sound of Slanty yelping in the night, running off down the street. Then he remembered he had bought dog biscuits along with the groceries. He ran downstairs, hoping to get the box before Eve saw it.

She pushed it at him scornfully. "Idiot! Why did you waste money on that? Maybe you'll be eating it by the end of the month! You haven't even got the dog!"

"I have to find him."

"What for? God! It's just like you—we may all wind up in the county home, and all you can think about is a stinking stray dog!"

"She kicked him. He may be hurt."

"What of it! There's a million stray dogs some-body may've kicked! Why don't you think about us for a change? What about Mom? What're we going to do?"

The sound of her voice, high and tight, as if she might cry, scared Brian as much as the questions. His eyes flickered from Eve to his mother, around the kitchen, to the box of dog biscuits on the table. He had to get out of there. He grabbed the box and ran out.

The screen door slammed. A fly buzzed around the kitchen. Eve stood and stared and felt her eyes water up and finally run over. She choked like a little girl and ran out of the room, up the stairs to the bathroom, where she could slam the door and cry by herself. What am I going to do? She rocked herself and sniffled and blew her nose. Somehow Brian was the last straw. He just didn't make sense. Her mother's drinking was bad enough—it was terrible—but you could put the groceries away, get the meals, sort of pretend to be the mother. But not with an idiot like Brian for a brother! He was old enough —you'd think he could be some help instead of always running off like a scared rabbit. She sniffled again, and got up to wash her face. There was something funny about the picture of Brian as a rabbit, even if he did make her mad. She heard Andy come up the stairs, so she finished fixing her face and combing out her hair and went into the hallway. She could see Andy standing in his room doing nothing. "How come Mom's sleeping in the kitchen?" he asked.

"Well, she just is. She's really passed out."

"Is she . . . sick? What's the matter?"

"Andy, you know. She's drunk."

"I thought people acted funny when they're drunk. They laugh or stumble around and tip chairs over, and they talk funny. Sometimes Mom does that."

"And sometimes they pass out. When people get drunk a lot, they're sick."

Andy's voice quavered. "When's she gonna get better?"

Eve thought, He's the one who looks like a scared rabbit now. Only he still looks like a little boy and you want to comfort him, not like Brian who runs off like he's sort of crazy. It struck her suddenly, maybe that was why her mother always seemed to baby Andy and get mad at Brian.

She put her hand on Andy's shoulder. "When she gets this bad, she usually gets sick—really sick, throwing up. Then she quits drinking and gets better. We'll get along, Andy. Brian got some food—I'll get supper pretty soon."

"O.K." Andy went past her into the bathroom.

Brian walked away from the house, keeping his mind firmly on the problem of finding the dog. He turned away from the park—he and Martha had looked there. He went down the side streets and into all the alleys, every time he saw a dog. It never turned out to be Slanty, and soon he would notice a person standing in a door looking at him suspiciously. When he got hungry, he opened the box of dog biscuits. They didn't taste bad. He remembered Eve saying he might have to eat them, but his mind veered away from that. He didn't want to think about home. He had to go on hunting for the dog.

He worked around to the east side of the park and found a street sign that said, To Vail Place. He'd never noticed that before. It was a rough, cobblestoned little street, and he saw two dogs ahead, but they didn't look like Slanty. He walked slowly along, watching the houses. They were occupied by black families. A black kid about his age came alongside him.

"Boy, what you doin down here?"

"Hunting for my dog. He's brown, with black ears, and sort of small."

"Ain't no dog like that down here." The glassy black eyes looked at Brian, expressionless, and he looked away.

"O.K., thanks."

Dwayne thumped Brian's shoulder. "Boy, what you thankin me for? I didn't find your dog. You goin give me a reward if I do?"

"Uh, sure." Brian turned away uneasily. He had a feeling the boy was kidding him.

"Listen here, you Brian . . ." Dwayne spoke patiently, almost in a fatherly tone. Brian stopped, surprised at hearing his name. ". . . jus turn round and look at me. I ain't goin fly way, I ain't goin disappear like a genie. Jus look at me. Now, what my name? You know it, you know you do."

Astonished at the easy tone of voice, Brian finally held his head up and looked right at Dwayne. He had seen him before. "Hey, ain't you . . ." Then his voice trailed off. He couldn't be sure.

"C'mon, you goin to get it. Think bout gym class. I trip over you and fell down, skin my knee last week. Lookit!" Dwayne pulled up his pant leg and showed the scab.

"Dwayne!" He did know. He could hear the kids and the coach shouting that name now. They shouted it all the time, because Dwayne was always doing something, but Brian had never really looked to see what face went with the name.

As he looked at him now, he made another discovery. "Say! I seen you the other day with Melvita."

"Sure nough. And you see me under that leather hat down to Soulard. I wink at you, and you look right through me. I bump into you in the schoolyard, and you don't even blink! You better get yo eyebrows up, boy!"

"Now I'll know. Next time I see you, I'll see you, like Martha."

"Hey, man, I ain't that big!"

"No, I just mean . . ."

"I gotta get home. See ya round. I be lookin for yo dog, too—what his name?"

"Slanty, I call him. He's brown . . ."

"Yeah, with black ears, I know. I be lookin out for him. Bye."

"Bye." Brian wondered where to go next, and then he remembered that it was Saturday again. The market would be open. Maybe a dog would go that way, where there was food.

When he got there, it was getting toward evening and the stalls were closing up. Brian stood idly watching a leathery faced farmer packing up his truck, with a boy helping him.

"Mister, you seen a dog? Little brown one with black ears?"

"I seen bout a million of everything—dawgs, people, pigeons, cars, trucks! Too much of everything in this city; time to go home. C'mon, Jim, leave the rest of them lettuces. They ain't no good, all wilted, we got better ones home."

The farmer went on talking as he worked, not really talking to Brian or to his son, just talking to help the work along.

"Mister, you need another boy down there on the farm to help with the work?" Brian could hardly believe that was his own voice. The idea just popped into his head as he watched the man working. He thought, I could work, and he'd take care of me, and everything would be all right.

The farmer stopped a moment and looked at Brian and smiled. The skin of his face folded into deep creases. His eyebrows were bleached almost white by the sun, and his eyes were bright.

"Sorry, son." The bubble burst, Brian looked away. The man said, "You go home, fatten up a bit, son. Maybe you work on a farm when you git older. Take long some of that lettuce to your mother. Soak it in cold water, it'll perk up. Bye now. C'mon, Jim."

The truck drove off and Brian stood there. There were old bags on the stall, and he picked one up and crammed in a few heads of lettuce and the dog biscuits. He'd just have to go on hunting. It was dark by the time he got back to Lafayette Park. His eyes flicked nervously into the shadows. He told himself he was hunting for Slanty, but really he looked into the dark corners because of the spooky fears running through his head. The tall houses seemed to look at him out of their blank windows, and they were old people, or ghosts. . . .

He saw three kids walking down the avenue, right in the middle of the street. When a car came, they got out of the way, but then they went right back out under the streetlights. They didn't walk on the shadowy sidewalk. Brian moved out there, too. He looked over toward the park and remembered to look for Slanty, but all he saw was one big silky dog on a leash being led into Benton Place, where the nice houses were and little foreign cars parked in front. It was nothing like Brian's street, though it was so close.

His feet were so tired he was almost used to them that way. He nibbled on another dog biscuit, but now it seemed too dry. He had to get something to drink. At last, he headed his feet toward home.

Long before he got there, he heard it, the rhythmic squeaking of the metal chair. So she was up, not asleep on the kitchen table anymore. At the foot of the porch stairs, he stopped and listened.

She was crooning to herself. "Think I don' know. . . . I know, can' fool me, unh-unh. . . . I see yuh sneakin' off. . . ."

Brian froze, thinking she was talking about him. She went on, but the words were just a blur, and he tiptoed up a step or two to look. Her back was to the stairs, jiggling up and down as she rocked the chair with her foot. She didn't have beer, she had a little juice glass in her hand. She took a tiny sip of the brown liquid; the chair stopped its squeaking.

"I know what yuh do . . . hide yuh money, tell me y' ain' got any . . . buy y' ticket and run home t' Momma. . . . She never like me." She laughed suddenly. "Y' momma saym no good, saym drunk." She laughed again. "Know what, Andrew? She right, heh, heh! She right, she can have yuh."

Brian stood glued to the step, listening. He realized now that she wasn't talking about him, she was talking about his father. His name was Andrew—Andy was named for him.

The squeaking of the chair and the crooning continued. "She can have yuh . . . can' have my baby . . . my baby's mine. . . . She got her Andy, I got my Andy, heh, heh . . ." The crazy laugh broke out again, scaring Brian, and then it suddenly changed to sobs. She was crying. She sniffled and the chair squeaked and Brian waited.

Finally he edged up the stairs. He looked down at her. Her eyes were half closed, and fat tears trickled down her cheeks. His fingers closed on his cold, sweaty palms, and he stiffened all over. Even her tears couldn't make him feel sorry for her. He couldn't think of her as an ordinary person, she just meant danger. He fumbled for the screen-door catch, and the door squeaked.

Her head snapped up, and her arm holding the glass knocked against the chair. The whiskey in it sloshed onto Brian's pants, and the smell hit his nose. Her eyes focused on him briefly. "Wha' yah want? Whe' yuh been? Think yuh can sneak past . . . I know . . . I know wha' yuh doing . . ."

Brian vanished into the kitchen, the door slammed, and there was silence until the squeak of the chair began again. Brian let his breath out slowly and relaxed. He went up the stairs and into his room. Andy was lying on his back in bed, and the streetlight shone in on his pale face.

His eyes opened, big and dark. "Brian?" he whispered.

"Yeah."

"Uh." Andy rolled over on his side, watching Brian as he sat down on his own bed and peeled his shoes and socks off. "Where you been?"

"Hunting for that dog I found. He ran away again."

"She won't let you keep him."

Brian didn't answer. Andy sniffed and wrinkled his nose. "What smells?"

"Your feet would smell too if you walked on them all day."

"It's not that."

"Her drink spilled on me." Brian took his jeans off and threw them into the far corner of the room.

"Brian?"

"Hunh?"

"What're we going to do?"

"I don't know." Brian was silent, but Andy continued to stare at him. Brian said, "Maybe she'll stop tomorrow."

"What if she doesn't?"

"Stay out of her way. Get out of the house." Brian rolled back on his bed and stretched out. He wasn't sleepy. He lay there, listening. In a little while, he heard Andy turn over, and without moving himself, he looked over. Andy was lying on his stomach now, with his face pressed into the mattress, and soon Brian heard the sound of quiet sniffling.

He lay stiffly on his back, staring at the ceiling. The sniffling went on.

"Andy?" Brian said finally.

"Unh?"

"It'll be all right. We'll manage."

"How?"

"Eve's big. And I can help. Until she stops. She's gotta stop sometime."

"Umm. Good night."

"Night." Brian waited and Andy stopped sniffling, and after a while Andy went to sleep. Brian lay and stared out at the streetlight. After listening to his mother, he felt differently about Andy somehow. The way she babied him, it was really all part of the way she was sick and drunk and mixed up. Just for a moment, he let himself wonder about his father—had he really left them and gone back to his mother? He sighed and turned over and shut his eyes. It was all too long ago. He slept.

chapter
seven

BRIAN WOKE UP as if he'd never moved, but now the sun was shining on his face. Slowly he raised his head. Andy's bed was empty, and the door was open. He listened. There was no sound. Gradually, he got his mind onto the new day and sat up. He put his feet on the floor. They still felt tired, and he saw that they were very dirty. He wiggled his toes and decided to take a shower. He hadn't done that in quite a while. He peeled off the shirt and underwear, which were also dirty, and found clean ones on Andy's side of the bureau.

When he got out of the shower, with his head

and everything dripping, he felt better. He remembered Slanty. Suddenly he was sure—today he would find him. His stomach rumbled, and he also remembered the bags of groceries he'd gotten yesterday. He hurried downstairs, but at the bottom paused warily to look around and listen. The sound of heavy, irregular breathing came from the front room. Brian peered in and relaxed. She was asleep on the sofa.

In the kitchen Andy had left milk and cereal spilled on the table, and there was the bag of wilted lettuce where he'd dropped it last night. He drew cold water into a pan, the way the man had said, and put the lettuce in to soak. He remembered he'd bought a can of tuna fish at the store the day before—it was dented, five cents off. His mouth watered at the idea of a real tuna fish sandwich with fresh lettuce.

Meanwhile he was ravenous. Andy had eaten about half the box of cold cereal, and Brian emptied the other half into a mixing bowl and covered it with milk and sugar. Afterward he made the sandwich and put it in the bag with the dog biscuits. He thought, We'll have a regular picnic, me and Slanty, when I find him. Then he thought, We'll need something to drink, and he found an empty jar and filled it with Kool-Aid.

He went up the street whistling softly under his breath. The street and the air seemed fresh and clean now. The houses around the park didn't look like staring old people anymore; they had become proper houses again, places to live.

He went past the vacant lot and looked at all the bushes high enough to hide a dog. He came to the first house, which was set far back from the street. It was small and narrow, like a house that had been sliced in half, and he'd hardly noticed it before, because it was set so far back and the bushes were so overgrown in front of it. As he looked at the house, something seemed to move. It was the curtain at the front window— someone had been looking out.

Brian's eyes dropped to the yard, traveled around the overgrown garden beds and the scraggly bushes, and stopped. There he was. There was Slanty.

Sitting under a bush, with the sun flickering on the leaves, he was almost invisible, his black ears and paws melting into the shadows. Brian whistled. The black ears pricked up, the head cocked a little on a slant.

Brian grinned. "Here, Slanty. Here, boy!" He squatted by the fence and reached into the paper bag. At the rustle of the paper, the dog stood up, his tail wagging slowly. Brian held out a dog biscuit. "Come on, boy!"

The dog came toward him slowly, the black end of his nose quivering. Finally he reached the biscuit in Brian's hand and took it carefully and neatly between his teeth. He moved back a little and crouched to eat it. Then he looked at Brian.

"More? Here, boy." He got out another biscuit, and another. The dog sat down now, and let Brian pet him. Brian wondered if he could get inside the yard. He looked up at the house again and saw the little triangle, where the curtain was held back at the corner of the window. Brian stayed very still and watched the watcher, but he couldn't tell who it was.

He petted Slanty again and tried not to think that someone owned the dog. "I didn't know where you were. I've been hunting for you all over, know it?"

The dog wagged his tail and sat down, his head still cocked, watching Brian.

"You're really mine, aren't you?" Brian went on. "I just keep you in this nice yard, where you're safe. O.K., Slanty?"

Suddenly the dog turned. The door to the house had opened. An old woman stuck her cane, one foot, and her head around the door and peered toward the street. "Who's that? Get away from there!" The voice tried to sound threatening, but it was too old. It was just the thin crackling of old tissue paper.

Brian stood up. "I'm just feeding the dog, ma'am."

The old woman edged out, but still held the door with one hand. Her head bobbed like one of those jiggling toys on a wire spring as she looked around the yard. "Here, Queenie, come here, dearie!"

The dog went to her, and the old lady went on talking. "That's my girl, come inside, dearie. Don't let those bad boys let you out in the street again. Did you get lost, dearie? I thought you'd been run over."

"Ma'am!" Brian called. "I won't let him out,

honest I won't. I'll just feed him and play with him."

"Eh?" She looked up, trying to focus on him. "Who's that?"

"My name's Brian. See, I came to play with the dog, ma'am. I won't hurt him."

"No one comes here. They've all gone away. Jamie's gone, Esther's gone, no one comes here anymore."

"Ma'am . . ." Brian called, but she had gone back inside, taking the dog with her.

Brian stood there. Now what? He tried to feel happy and excited that he'd found Slanty, but somehow he couldn't. Slanty wasn't a stray dog, he belonged to someone, and Brian couldn't take care of him or go on a picnic with him. There was nothing to do with the whole day now.

Martha. He ought to tell her he'd found the dog. He picked up his bag and walked around to her house. There were no babies playing out front and no sound of voices and TV from the house. Brian walked up to the front door uneasily. Why was no one around?

He knocked. He knew—no one was home. He walked back out to the sidewalk and stood there disconsolate. Could they have all gone away, just like that? If Martha had gone, he didn't know what he'd do.

A set of church bells rang, and then another and another. Brian grinned and straightened up. It was Sunday, that was all. They must have gone to church. She'd said something about that.

He'd have to think of something else to do for a while.

He remembered Dwayne. He didn't know where the kid lived, but that was something he knew how to do, hunt. If he'd found one little stray dog, it must be easier to find a boy.

He walked away from the park. There was his own street, Rutger—Dwayne didn't live there. He came to Caroline Street and turned down that. It was about like his own street, some houses looking pretty good, some shabby, some boarded up. He came to one with a side porch like his own. There was a middle-aged black man standing out front, looking up at the peeling paint. The porch ran along the ground floor and along the second story, too, and there were lines of laundry up there.

"Dwayne! Hey, boy, come out here!" the man shouted. Brian grinned. See, this is my lucky day. I've found him.

Dwayne came out the door, head down, looking sullen. His father walked with him alongside the house, running his hand over some of the cracked paint and pointing to bare patches up above. He had a scraping tool in his hand which he gave to Dwayne. Dwayne looked at the tool and swore. His father said, "Don't bad mouth that tool, boy—use it! I'll get the ladder."

From the sidewalk, Brian called. "Hey, Dwayne, hi!" Dwayne looked up, and Brian went on, "I didn't know where you lived, but I found it! I found my dog, too."

"Ain't that fine," Dwayne muttered. He ran

the scraper over the alligator-hide paint on the porch and enjoyed the ugly rasping noise it made. The paint chips flew up in his face and he cussed at that. He was cross enough being waked up on Sunday morning and dragged out to scrape paint, without having some kid watching, probably laughing, talking about his silly old dog. Because he wanted to be angry anyway, Dwayne let himself run on. He muttered, What that white boy want to come snoopin round here for, see how I live?

Dwayne's father came out, puffing as he balanced a long, heavy ladder. He came well out toward the sidewalk with one end and set it down, before trying to get the other end up against the porch.

"I could help," Brian said. He surprised himself and surprised Dwayne's father, too.

"Mornin, son," he said carefully. "You friend of Dwayne's?"

"Yeah, we're in school together."

"Dwayne, how come you don't int'rduce me to your friend? Where your tongue, boy?"

"In my head, long with a bunch a paint chips!" Dwayne snapped. "That there is Brian! He come round to watch me work!"

"He say he want to help." Mr. Yale turned away from his son and spoke confidentially to Brian. "Don't mind him, Brian. He just get out the wrong side of bed this morning, and he not too enthoo-siastic bout painting the porch. But he come round, after he work his mad off. You want to work, for real?"

"Sure."

"Stay right there—don't go way. I get nother scraper." He came back with a putty knife. "This do O.K. You climb up on the ladder there, and don't drop nothin on your friend, Dwayne! Don fall off the ladder, I ain't got no insurance. Squinch up yo eyes so you don't get paint chips in 'em."

Brian climbed up and started prying at the paint, slowly and carefully. He'd never used tools much—Andy was the one who did things like that at home. Down below, Dwayne scraped at his paint even more furiously, and chips flew out in a cloud around him. Mr. Yale watched the two of them. He grinned and then he started to shake with silent laughter. He hurried inside, shut the door, and told his wife: "I got this skinny little white boy up on the ladder scrapin paint down on Dwayne, and Dwayne so mad he could eat tacks! He so mad he goin to get the house scraped in jig time!"

"You didn't ought to torment Dwayne like that."

"Ain't tormentin nobody. White boy say he want to help, and I give him a tool, that's all I done. He might not chip as much paint as Dwayne do, but he be a fine gadfly!" Mr. Yale started laughing again.

After half an hour, Dwayne was dripping with sweat and he'd settled down to methodical scraping. He hadn't spoken to Brian yet but he really wasn't angry anymore. Finally he put his own scraper down and stood back to see what Brian was doing. Brian didn't look hot and he'd cleared a small patch of paint with careful little wrist motions.

"Man, that ain't no silver you polishing! You can beat on it," Dwayne said.

"I never did it before—I guess I don't know how."

"Oh, you doin all right; don't worry, you get the hang of it. You want a cold drink?"

"O.K."

Dwayne brought sodas out and they leaned against the house in the shade to drink. Halfway through, Dwayne started to laugh.

"What's funny?"

"It sure nough tickle me, you scrapin paint on my house!"

Brian didn't really see the joke, but he didn't mind. He was drinking in the unaccustomed pleasure of sharing a soda and a job with another kid.

They went back to work, and as the sun got really hot even Brian had color in his face and sweat in his hair. Mrs. Yale called to them. "You boys ready for some lunch?"

Dwayne dropped his tool instantly. Brian climbed down the ladder and picked up his lunch bag where he'd left it. He said, "I got my sandwich. See, I was going to have a picnic."

"Picnic? C'mon, my momma got plenty lunch."

They went inside and he said, "Momma, this here's Brian."

She said, "Afternoon, Brian. Sit down here. We havin some spaghetti and meatballs. It be leftovers, but it real good."

"Uh—thank you, ma'am. I've got my sandwich here."

"Aw, throw it away—give it to your dog," Dwayne said.

Brian exclaimed, "It's a real good sandwich! It's tuna fish, and this man down at Soulard gave me a lot of fresh lettuce."

Dwayne rolled his eyes and started, "Aw . . ."

Mrs. Yale interrupted easily. "You have your sandwich, Brian, and maybe then you like some spaghetti and meatballs, too. That be nice."

In fact Brian had no trouble going through the sandwich, the spaghetti, two glasses of milk, and cake and Jell-O. Dwayne ate almost as much, but carelessly, leaving bits on his plate. Mrs. Yale exchanged a quick glance with her husband and then took care not to watch Brian openly.

The boys worked in the afternoon until they got too hot. Dwayne said, "C'mon, we go down to Jack's and get us some ice sticks."

"Uh . . ." Brian hesitated, remembering he had no money.

"Hey, Pop, what you goin to pay us for all that work we did?" Dwayne stuck his head inside the back door.

Mr. Yale reached in his pocket and got out four quarters. "That be on account—you get some more when you through for real."

Brian looked astonished when Dwayne handed him fifty cents. "Gee . . ."

Dwayne snorted. "Maybe he ain't got much today. You come back nother day, we get the rest."

They stood in front of Happy Jack's licking on their ices. Terry and Jasper and a few other kids came by, and their eyes slid curiously over Brian standing there with Dwayne.

"You comin to play ball?" Terry said to Dwayne.

"O.K. I got to get my glove. Meet you there." He started off, then remembered Brian. "You wanta come?"

"Thanks. I ain't much good at ball. I gotta go feed my dog."

Terry snickered to Jasper in a singsong: "He ain't much good at ball, at all!" Dwayne glared at him briefly, and then he waved to Brian and went off to get his glove.

Brian walked away slowly. He was tired after all the unaccustomed work and the big lunch. He thought of going up to see Slanty. On the corner of Rutger Street he paused, undecided.

He heard a siren in the distance. There were always sirens. City Hospital was right down the avenue. The siren grew loud and shrill and then the sound filled the whole place, as it turned off Park Avenue and down Eighteenth. It came right at Brian and he stepped back involuntarily —the ambulance slowed and heeled at the corner and went down Rutger Street. The siren turned off, the noise whirred into silence.

Daydreamy, frozen in his tracks, Brian followed it with his eyes. You couldn't not watch an ambulance going down your own street. He still didn't react when the ambulance slowed and pulled to a stop on the right. His house. The movie rolled on, without any sound now, as two little white figures got out of the ambulance and went to the house. They came back, little white legs twinkling, and carried a stretcher to the house. Back again, carrying the stretcher, heavy now. They put it in the ambulance. They drove away. Before they rounded the far corner, the siren whirred into life again, loud, then diminishing into the distance. Just a siren, Brian tried to think, nothing to do with me. But his heart knew different, it was beginning to pound, and his feet were hurrying down the street.

The kitchen door squeaked open under his hand and Andy and Eve looked at him.

"What happened?" Brian said.

"Where have you been?" Eve exploded.

"Mom?" Brian looked around vaguely, expecting to see or hear her.

Andy said, "I was out on the porch, and I heard this thud. She fell on the floor. She was so white, and her head was bleeding. Eve called the hospital."

Brian looked at Eve, and she sighed and slumped over the table. "Yeah. She really passed out. She was drinking all day. I don't know where she got so much stuff. I hid one bottle, but she had another."

"She looked awful," Andy said, almost whispering, his eyes big and his mouth trembly.

"Is she . . . is she . . . ?" Brian started over. "What did they say, the ambulance guys?"

"They didn't say much. They were just young guys," Eve said.

Andy said, "He asked where our daddy was, and Eve said he was working."

"Well, I didn't want him getting nosy about us—they don't like it if there's no adult at home. I asked him about Mom, but he said I'd have to call the hospital."

"He listened to her heart was all," Andy said. "With that thing around his neck, the stethoscope. That's what they call it."

Brian stood there, looking down at the top of Andy's head, where the cowlick sprouted up. Eve stared at the table, and Andy looked back at the TV. Brian felt terribly tired, suddenly hardly able to stand up. He stumbled across the hall into the living room. That was the last place he'd seen her. When he went out this morning, she'd been asleep on the couch. He flung himself down there now and buried his face in the cushions. A terrible relief flooded him, that she was gone, and then a terrible fear that she wouldn't come back. His mind blacked out the two fears and he fell asleep.

When he woke up and went back to the kitchen, no one was there but the TV, still talking to itself. He turned it off. That was better, quiet. He got a glass of water and went out on the porch. It was still light out. As he sat down on the metal chair, it let out its squeak, and he jumped, frightened. He stood up and listened.

Everything in the house was silent. Out of habit, Brian went down the steps and along the street. He could think better walking. He walked toward the old lady's house, where he'd found the dog.

chapter
eight

SLANTY WAS OUTSIDE under his bush, and he came right to Brian. He knew him now. Brian slid down, leaned against the fence, and petted the dog and talked to him, a singsong murmur, not really saying anything.

"Boy! What you doin here? You ain't tell me you find your dog!"

It was Martha, and Brian jumped. His mind had been miles away, and now he looked up and there she was standing with her hands on her big hips, grinning down at him.

"Yeah, I found him. Where you been all day? I looked for you."

"I been at church. All day. They be havin the June gatherin. They have lunch an' an afternoon service and the choir singin and everythin. I get home and my momma ask me to peel some potatoes and I run outta the house so I won't scream at her. I can't stand to see no more *food!*"

"Yeah? You know what—I ate lunch with Dwayne. His mom cooks really good stuff, spaghetti and cake . . ."

"Don't talk about it! Tell me where you find this ole dog and what he doin in ole Maisie's yard?"

"Uh, well, I found him here." Brian paused. "I'm going to keep him here. It's a good place, sort of shady, see . . ."

"Boy, who is you kiddin? This here house belong to crazy Maisie, all the kids know that. See, there she be, peekin at you out the window. She always do that. And this got to be her dog. It in her yard, ain't it?"

"Well . . ." Brian looked up at the old lady's window and saw the curtain held back. ". . . she knows me now. I talked to her, and she's going to let me keep him here. He likes me. Don't you, Slanty boy? Here, boy. See, he comes to me, even when I don't have food."

Martha sighed. "All right, you can 'tend he be yo dog, and you jus don't have the bother of him at home. She let you go in the yard?"

"Uh, sure." He looked up. The curtain had dropped back in place now. They went into the yard and sat under the little tree, where Slanty had dug himself a little hollow.

"You want me to tell you what I do all day?" Martha said. "Maybe I tell you, I stop thinkin bout it."

"What'd you do?"

"Not eat, that what. Just not eat, seem like the whole day. See, everyone bring the thing they like best to cook to the church. My momma bring some pork and gravy and a coconut frosting cake, mmm-mmm!"

"I had chocolate frosting cake," Brian said.

"They pull the Sunday-school tables together, and everybody put out they dish. Then everybody go round and pile up they plate. That where my trouble begin.

"I didn take no pork and gravy, no ham, no chittlins, no macaroni cheese, no potato salad. Just a little bitty bit of cottage cheese and collards and lettuce and tomato, floatin round on a great big empty plate.

"Then the sister cuttin the ham, she say, 'Martha, didn you hear the preacher? He say, Bless this food to our use! Don't hold back, girl— you goin do the Lord' work. You just got nough food for a rabbit on that plate.'

"An I say, 'Yes, ma'am, I be comin back for more later. I gotta get Katie started.' And Katie start yellin she want coconut cake and I tell her we get it later.

"Then we sit down. Usually I get a whole lot to eat and I talk a lot, you know me, so it all take a whole lot of time, and it be fun. But today I ain't got nuthin to eat and nuthin to say, and in two minutes my plate empty. Flat, shiny empty.

Katie still eating. Finally she finish and she say,
'We gettin our cake now? I wan ice cream, too!'

"And I snap, 'You can get your own! You big
nough!' Katie stick her lip out and she think I'm
mad at her, and I feel bad, so I gotta go help
her. I come back with a little piece of water-
melon for me.

"Sister sitting cross from me, she say, 'I bet
you be dieting, right?'

" 'No, ma'am.'

" 'Child, you don't need to worry. That just be
puppy fat, you goin lose it soon nough!' That
what she say. That what they all say—puppy
fat! Huh! Pig fat, that what it be!" Martha
scowled and stopped.

Brian tried to think what it would be like to
worry about eating too much, but he couldn't
really imagine it.

Martha laughed. "O.K., I got rid of my
troubles; how you doin? Your momma get any
better?"

Just the word momma tore into him. He'd forgotten, but now it all came back. He stared
down at the ground, and his arms hung limp.

"What the matter?" Martha asked.

"They took her to the hospital."

"Uh-oh, that bad! When they do that?"

" 'Safternoon."

"Maybe it ain't so bad, really. They stop her
drinking and get her all fixed up again, before
they send her home. They do that with Katie's
daddy once."

"Maybe she's dead even."

"Don't talk like that! She couldn't be dead without you knowin. They tell you."

"There was only the ambulance men, and they didn't say much. Maybe they don't know."

"Sure, they know! They can tell if someone dead—you know on TV, the doctor or someone take one look, and then he shake his head. He know."

"That's on TV."

"Well, look, maybe you hear people say someone is 'dead drunk.' But that don't mean they dead—just real bad drunk. They get over it."

"She drank about three bottles of whiskey, Eve said. Maybe you don't get over that."

"Well, Eve's big! She can do for you, and everything be all right till your momma get back. You got food in the house?"

"Yeah, we got food yesterday. Her check came, and she cashed it. I guess that's how come she got so much liquor. We ain't got much food, but we got some. Pretty soon, I guess it'll run out." He looked as if it all really had nothing to do with him.

Martha stamped her foot. "You get yoself together, boy! Don't act like it ain't none of yo business. You got to help your sister! You be big, too—she ain't got to do everythin!"

Brian looked at her blankly. "What can I do?"

"Well, you can help! Some way. Like, maybe you can earn a little money running an errand. Anyway, you best stay round home, see if she need you stead of mooning around here with

96

this old dog. He don't need you—he just a dog in a yard. He got someone to take care of him."

"Mmm." Brian stood up reluctantly. "Bye, bye, Slanty. I'll come back."

"Hmmph! Ain't nothin to him, whether you come back or not!"

Brian's head snapped up. "It does, too! He knows me! He loves me—lookit, see how he looks at me?"

"Aw, any ole dog do . . ." Martha started, and then she saw how much Brian needed to think the dog loved him. "Well, I guess he do. But yo sister and brother, they be needin you more. They is people, don't you know that?"

Martha took him by the arm. "Come on, you can walk me home, fore you go on home yo own self. If yo sister need somethin, you come on back and tell me. My momma always got plenty of potatoes, stuff like that."

"O.K.," Brian said. He left Martha and walked on home. Eve and Andy were sitting in the kitchen, not talking or eating or even watching television.

"How come you always got to sneak off?" Eve complained. "The minute I take my eye off you, you disappear!"

"What's happening?"

"I just want to tell you, anyway. I called the hospital, and they said I could come down this evening, and maybe I can talk to the doctor. So you stay here with Andy."

Brian looked at Andy blankly. Automatically, Brian said, "What for?"

"Oh, don't be stupid!" Eve stormed. "You ought to *be* here, that's all!"

"All right."

Andy said, "The hospital, they said she's on the critical list. That means she's bad, but she's going to get better. Doesn't it?"

"Mmm. Yeah," Brian said.

They got some supper and Eve went to the hospital. Brian and Andy sat there in the kitchen, half looking at the television, so they wouldn't ask each other any questions. When Eve came back, they both swung around and Andy actually turned off the TV. It was like telling the machine to go away, because now, finally, they really had to listen to each other.

Eve leaned against the refrigerator. "They didn't tell me much really. I saw her and she's breathing all right but she's still unconscious."

"Unconscious, that's just like sleeping." Andy stated it confidently. "When she wakes up, she'll be O.K."

He looked at Eve for assurance, but she turned and opened the refrigerator door and tried to believe she was hungry. It would be reassuring to feel hungry. But she didn't. She pulled out the pitcher of Kool-Aid and poured some into a glass.

Brian watched the bright green liquid, but he could feel Andy looking at him. Andy said, "She's gonna be all right when she wakes up, right?"

"I guess," Brian said. "Don't worry, Andy." He said it, but he knew Andy was still like a little kid; if he didn't know where his mother was, his world fell apart. Brian and Eve could sort of remember a time when they felt mothered, but it was a long time ago. For quite a while they had known there was really no mother in that house, only trouble. You could try to avoid it.

"You coming to bed?" Andy asked, and they could hear the tremble in his voice. He'd never paid any attention before to when Brian went to bed.

"Yeah, come on. Night, Eve."

"Night, Eve," Andy said.

"Night," Eve said. She listened to their feet on the stairs and realized she had never bothered to say good night to her brothers before.

chapter
nine

IN THE MORNING, Eve drank coffee, Brian ate peanut butter on toast, and Andy had cold cereal. They didn't talk—they were each half asleep, half getting ready for the push to school.

Eve called the hospital, but the operator said to call later. She came back to the kitchen and saw Brian getting dog biscuits out of the cupboard. "You going to school?" she asked.

He stuffed a few biscuits in his pocket hurriedly. "O.K.," he said.

"I don't care if you go or not! If you want to

hunt for that dumb dog, I suppose you will. You could stay home, in case the hospital called."

"I'll go to school." Brian realized he'd never even told them he had found Slanty.

Eve sniffed. "I'm going to school, too. I'd go crazy waiting around here, and I can phone from there. See you this afternoon."

She went off, and Andy and Brian shuffled in their seats. Even though their mother didn't talk much in the morning, they both felt how strange it was in the house now. There was a spooky stillness.

"Let's go, huh?" Andy said.

"O.K."

They went up the street. Two little kids were playing in a yard near the corner. The little boy looked at them and said, "I see th'ambulance yestiddy." Then he made a siren noise and ran across the yard.

The little girl, a bit older, stared at them. "Your momma sick, ain't she?"

"Uh-huh," Andy grunted.

The little girl smiled slyly. "My momma say she ain't sick, she drunk."

"Nosy dumb kid," Brian muttered.

"When you think Mom's coming home, huh, Brian?" Andy asked.

"Few days I guess."

"They don't let her drink any of that stuff in the hospital, see," Andy said. "So after a few days, she gets all right."

"Uh-hunh."

"She won't even *want* to drink that stuff anymore, when she gets home. See, in the hospital there's this doctor. He's young . . . no, maybe he's older. He's real serious but, you know— nice. He talks to her. He tells her this stuff is like poison for some people. That's true—I seen it on TV. So she listens and she decides she won't drink any more stuff, it could kill her . . ."

Brian thought, Yeah, on TV nothing really bad ever happens to the kid who's the hero. His mother couldn't even be a drunk.

"Then this doctor . . . you know, you can tell, he really likes her, too. So he brings her home himself and . . ."

What if she doesn't come home? What if she does die? Brian shocked himself enough to stop walking for an instant. Andy looked at him, questioning.

"Got something in my eye," Brian muttered and fell into step again. What really shocked him, though, was that when he thought she might die, he didn't really feel anything. Just blank. Why can't I be like Andy, cry, or get scared or something? On television, if anyone is sick or dies the others are always crying and moaning and screaming. Why don't I?

"Brian? I can't even remember our daddy, can you?"

Brian reached out and touched Andy lightly on the shoulder. It was a relief to feel Andy's body—solid and real. "Yeah, I remember him. Just barely."

"He ain't coming back ever, hunh?"

"Nah."

"I'll meet you here after school, O.K.? Eve's gonna call them up, and then they'll tell her when Mom can come home."

"Yeah, O.K."

When they got home that afternoon, Eve was already there. "I'm just going to call," she said. "If you're going anywhere, you wait! You wait till I find out."

He and Andy stayed in the kitchen and listened.

"I'm inquiring about Mrs. Jane Moody," she said. There was a pause and she repeated it.

"Who is calling?" the hospital desk asked.

"This is her daughter."

"Mrs. Moody is off the critical list. Her condition is good."

"Do you know when she can come home?"

"I have no release date yet. Hold on, please." There was silence, and the call was transferred to another hospital worker. "Will you be coming for Mrs. Moody?"

"Yes," Eve said.

"Your name, please?"

"Eve Moody."

"Age?"

Eve thought the voice sounded suspicious. Smoothly she said, "Nineteen."

"Is there another adult at home?"

"Uh . . . no."

"Younger children?"

"They're staying with my aunt." She was surprised at how easily the safe answers came out.

"Very well, Miss Moody. Please phone Extension 204 at nine A.M. tomorrow."

"Yes, ma'am." Eve put down the phone and let out a great sigh. It was going to be all right. She realized she hadn't just been afraid about her mother. She was afraid they'd ask questions. Maybe the hospital would send a social worker and take the boys away. She couldn't stand that. She'd never really thought she was fond of them —at least, not since Andy was a baby and cute and she could feed him. Now, suddenly, they were close together.

She went back to the kitchen and told them. "She's better. Maybe she'll come home tomorrow."

"Hot dog! I knew it! I knew the doctor could do it!" Andy whooped.

Brian thought, So he was right. It's like his TV plot. Then he thought about her coming home, and the old feeling of dread tightened up his stomach.

It was two days before Mrs. Moody came home. When Brian came back from school, he knew she'd be home. She was sitting inside the living room, not in the familiar squeaky porch chair or watching TV in the kitchen.

Brian was startled. "Uh, hi, Mom. You feel O.K. now?"

"Yes, I'm fine." She looked at him, and he knew she saw him all right—she even half smiled. But something was wrong. He felt as if she was a different person, a stranger. Her face didn't have the familiar expressions.

She was knitting. She'd never done that before, and she looked down, peering at the stitches and moving her hands awkwardly.

"I didn't know you knew how to knit," Brian said.

"I used to," she said, from a long way away. "One of the hospital people gave me some needles and started me again."

"Yeah, that's good. It's something to do."

"I can make Andy a cap for winter," she said.

"Uh-huh." Brian turned away and went uncertainly into the kitchen. He wondered if he should stay around, or say something more to her. After a while he went to the cupboard. He got some dog biscuits and went out.

Now, when Brian came home she was sitting in that same place knitting. The room was rather dark, even in the daytime, and she had one light shining on her hands, where her index finger wiggled with the wool. The radio no one used to play was on the table beside her, turned on now, a steady tinkling and talking. Brian would pause at the door and look into her private world.

"Uh, hi, Mom."

"Oh!" She'd look up as if surprised that he was home. "Is school out?"

"Yeah."

She'd look at the radio. "That's right, he said it was three o'clock."

Brian would wander up to his room and lie on the bed dozing or reading comics. Later, he'd hear Eve come in and his mother in the kitchen fixing supper. She took more time about it now, not just opening cans, but peeling potatoes and stirring up a pudding. She sat at the table and ate with them. There was always a tense quiet moment when she reached out to take a pill from the little bottle that sat beside the salt. Brian hadn't asked what they were. He knew she'd brought them home from the hospital.

He couldn't shake the feeling that something was different about her. Not just that she wasn't drinking, but that she was a different person, as if the doctor had changed something inside her.

"What are you going to do this summer, Brian?" she asked one night at supper. The simple question suddenly terrified him; she had never asked anything like that before. It was as if she didn't know him.

"Uh, I'll be around, I go to the library sometimes," he muttered.

It seemed to him she looked at him as if she expected something more, but the moment passed because Andy interrupted. "I'm gonna be on the Boys' Club baseball team. They're gonna take us swimming, too, out in the state park."

"I think I've got a job," Eve said. "Down at Ralston. I'll find out this week."

Brian thought, I've got Slanty. I can go feed him and play with him and maybe we'll go somewhere. But down inside, he knew this wasn't a plan for the summer, the way Andy and Eve had plans. For sure, it wasn't a plan he could tell his mother. Feeling somehow guilty he tried to slink out the door after supper.

"Where you going, Brian?" his mother called in her new, polite voice.

"Just out. I'll be back."

Eve saw her mother's face tighten and noticed the way she cleared the table and set the pots in the sink with quick, irritated movements. Eve thought, Why does he have to act like that? Always sort of queer and not telling anyone anything? It came back to her then, a quick picture from childhood: the screen door slamming behind her father, his voice calling, "Just out," and the hard line of her mother's mouth.

Brian sat quietly through the last days of school. After the weeks of trouble at home, his mother getting worse, then going to the hospital, the walking around the city hunting for Slanty, he was content just to sit and flip magazines or draw or do crosswords. The other kids played checkers and made things and gossiped together —Mr. Cousins didn't mind so long as they were quiet.

On the last day of school, when the other kids burst into the street shouting and hurraying, Brian drifted off by himself to old Maisie's yard, to talk to Slanty. That put off going home.

When he did get home, he saw his mother and Andy on the back porch. She was putting something on his head, and he squirmed and giggled. "It tickles!"

"Put your hands down—you'll make me drop stitches!" she said, laughing, too. "Look, it fits!"

"Lemme see, lemme go in the bathroom!" Andy said.

"No, you've got to wait for Christmas, you can't see," she teased and put the cap behind her back.

Brian came up the steps, and he saw her face change. "Oh, where have you been?" she said.

"Uh . . ." But there was nothing to tell her, so he said what he'd really been thinking. "Are you going to knit something for me?"

She shrugged. "You! You'd lose your head if it wasn't tied on!"

"Yeah, dopey!" Andy said. "Where's my Cards T-shirt you took?"

"It's upstairs, you never looked!" Brian punched him.

His mother snapped, "What're you hitting him for? Did you take his shirt?"

"Aww!" Brian went inside and let the door slam. Somehow he felt angry all over, and yet there was nothing really to be angry at.

There were hot dogs and potato salad for supper that night, and his mother served out a plate for each of them. Eve jumped up and flipped off the TV. "We don't need that thing on all the time! I got the job at Ralston. I'm going to start next week. I went down—you should see that office! It's got carpets and everything, and the girls really look neat!"

"We're gonna get uniforms for our team," Andy said.

The meal went on, with Andy and Eve doing the talking. Once Brian's mother said to him,

"Why don't you go down to the club, too? There're kids your age."

"I don't like to play ball."

She didn't say anything more, but he felt as if there was something wrong with him.

After supper, he remembered he hadn't seen Martha in a while, not since the night his mother went to the hospital. Of course, he'd seen her at school, but they hadn't really talked. He walked down to her house.

"Hey, Brian, where you been at?" Martha was out front with Katie. "School, you be lookin at me like you don't see me again. What kind of carryin on is that?"

"I don't know. I must of been thinking about something,"

"You tell me yo momma home. She O.K. now, ain't she? They get her off that stuff and she don't drink no more?"

"Yeah. She's knitting now."

Martha laughed. "Well, that be good! She knit you socks, keep your feet warm in winter!"

"She ain't knitting nothing for me. She's knitting Andy a cap."

"Oh, well, after that, she knit you somethin."

"Unh-unh. She won't."

"What you mean? You crazy, boy! She didn't tell you that, now did she? You jus makin it up."

"Mmm . . . well, maybe she didn't, but she treats me funny, like I'm a stranger. She doesn't like me. I know."

"You is really something else! You know that

first time you come over here, and you say 'I hate my momma'—well, she be drinkin then, maybe you got a reason. Now she ain't drinkin, and you say she don't like you. Boy, you is all mixed up!"

"How do I know when she's gonna be drinking and when she's not? Besides . . ." He paused, trying to think what he really meant. From inside the house he heard Martha's mother scolding someone. "Listen," he said, "you got a lot of kids in your family. Which one does your mother like best? Which one does she pick on?"

"She don't do like that! She don't like no one the best. Sometime she talk sweet to me, sometime she fuss. Same with all the others. It all come out even in the end."

"It doesn't come out even with me," Brian said.

"Aww . . ." Martha started to argue with him, but then she looked at his face and stopped. Maybe a kid and his mother just can't get along, just always rub each other the wrong way, specially if she be sometime drunk and sometime not. My momma, she be always the same, you can count on her. My daddy, too. Be hard on Brian, with no daddy home. Lotsa kids got no daddy. Melvita don't. Guess I be lucky. . . .

Brian interrupted her thinking. "What're you gonna do all summer, Martha?"

"I don know. There ain't much. Cept me and Katie going to Illinois to visit for a couple of weeks."

Brian thought, Guess that leaves me and Slanty.

chapter
ten

AFTER SCHOOL let out, Dwayne got down to painting the part of the house he and Brian had scraped. His father said, "Where yo skinny little friend? He need another meal—you better get him to help you."

"I didn't see him in a while," Dwayne said. "I don't know where he live. Jus have to wait till he turn up again." Actually, he didn't mind painting alone, and he wanted to earn as much money as he could. By the Fourth of July weekend, he had the job all done. The ladder and paint were put away and the yard all raked.

"There! Now it be lookin pretty when your gran'momma come," his mother said.

His father paid him ten dollars and offered to drive them all to Six Flags Park on Sunday. Melvita came along, and for once Dwayne could spend money freely. By the end of the day, he'd spent it all, but he didn't let Melvita know that.

Melvita had never been out of the city in a car before. She exclaimed over everything, the Interstate highway and the billboards and factories, and train cars alongside the highway piled high with automobiles. As they came back into the suburbs close to St. Louis, she sat up straight and pointed. "Man, lookit all the parks they got and all them big houses!"

"That ain't no park, girl! It jus the backyard go with that house."

"Backyard? They playin baseball in there!"

"So. They rich folks, don't you know that?"

"Mmm, that what I want when I get my house. I'm goin to have me a big backyard, and you can play baseball in it, and I look out the window, and I know where you be, all the time!"

"Them houses ain't for people like us."

"I know." She sighed and leaned against him and closed her eyes.

After a few minutes, she opened her eyes and looked at Dwayne. "Hey—how they figure out who goin to get the big house with the baseball field, and who goin to get the house with the plaster cracked and the broken glass out back? How they decide that, huh?"

Up front, Dwayne's father laughed shortly.

"Some cats make all the rules. They the ones get the big houses, don't you worry, girl!"

Melvita sat up straight and set her chin. "Well, then, when I grow up, I goin to be there when they make the rules."

"They don't let chicks make laws," Dwayne scoffed.

"You wait. They didn see me yet!"

Dwayne, in spite of himself, looked at her admiringly. "Yeah, they see you comin, they better get under the seat!"

"Right on, brother!" Melvita settled back comfortably in the seat again. "What you goin to do next week, Dwayne?"

There it was, the same old question. Automatically, Dwayne answered, "Hunt me a job."

The next week passed, and he did a few jobs for neighbors, raking a yard, hauling some trash, repairing a back step, but he hardly made more money than he spent every night at Happy Jack's. On Saturday, his mother kept him busy around the house all morning, and then she gave him two quarters. He went away scowling, thinking, That ain't pay, that jus a handout. Then he felt bad, because she was his mother, and he knew she didn't have money to spare.

He walked away from home, over toward the park. The boys were playing ball in there, but Dwayne walked past stiff-faced. He was still angry about the hassle the day before. They ruled him out on a base, when he knew he was safe. He was the pitcher, and they should have known he was right. They could just see who they'd get to pitch now—he wasn't going to play.

He saw Melvita and Martha sitting on a bench in the playground. He could always tell Melvita's funny hair sticking up, with a piece of yarn tied in it. He felt good, thinking she was his girl. He jingled the two quarters in his pocket—at least he'd have something to spend with her tonight.

Meanwhile, there was all day to spend, and he wasn't going to spend it sitting in the park baby-sitting. He walked on past the City Hospital and the project houses. He looked up at them, with all the broken windows gaping or boarded up, and he was glad he didn't live there.

They had a big new recreation building down there though, on Twelfth Avenue. Maybe I get in a game down there, he thought. I can pitch better than them project dudes.

He sauntered alongside the field, as if he wasn't much interested, and yelled to a boy he knew, a little guy built like a monkey: "Hey, Calvin! You winnin?"

"What else? Man, I don't lose! You wanta play?"

"I don't care. Ain't got my glove."

"Wait till next inning. I tell Mole."

Calvin used to live near Dwayne, and they used to hang out together then. Calvin used to catch when Dwayne pitched.

Mole was the dude pitching on this team. Dwayne knew him by sight. He was a couple of years older, and baad! Dwayne felt the skin on

the back of his neck prickling, and he thought,
That one cat I won't never mess with. I don't tell
him I be the pitcher.

At the end of inning, Mole's team was gathered in their dugout. Mole stood there, slapping
the ball into his glove, but his eyes ranged over
the field, the other players, and Dwayne. Dwayne
let their eyes meet but kept his own bland and
expressionless while he joked with a boy near him.
Mole could think what he wanted about him.

"Hey, Willie!" Mole called. It was an order.
"This cat Dwayne going to play third base for a
while. Loan him your glove."

"Good, I done been out in this sun long
enough," Willie said, and tossed his glove to
Dwayne.

Third base, Dwayne thought, that ain't my
spot. But when they went out in the field, he got
the picture: Mole could watch him all the time.
A runner got to second and Mole's eyes bored in
on him, testing, seeing if he would get nerved up.
Mole pegged the ball to him, hard, but Dwayne
caught it easily, tossed it home, kicked his base
carelessly. On the next play, he got the runner
out.

They played a few more innings, and Mole's
team won. Everyone was hot, so they went into
the rec building for drinks. Dwayne got a soda
and a candy bar, and then he and Calvin played
Ping-Pong.

"Pretty nice joint you got here," Dwayne said.
"Yeah, we going to have us a basketball team
in winter. You play?"

"I might. I see if I can fit it in!" Dwayne grinned and served the Ping-Pong ball. He won the game.

Mole sauntered up and watched the last few points. Calvin laid down his paddle, and Mole said, "You settin up to be champ?"

"If you say so," Dwayne said.

"I ain't sayin, you got to show me."

They started playing and right away Dwayne knew Mole could beat him. He played along easily, winning a few points, but losing more. Once he got Mole way back from the table and then dropped a soft one just over the net.

Calvin laughed and Mole threw him one of those squinty looks, and after that Mole didn't miss any more points. He put his paddle down and said, "You might come along, boy. With practice. Like, you might get to be second best!"

"Man, I don't practice to be second best. This just ain't my game, dig?"

"What yo game, man?"

"Oh-h—" Dwayne rocked back on his heels and cupped the one quarter in his pocket, then walked jauntily over to the soda machine and got another soda. Now he only had a dime left —Melvita would be out of luck tonight. He walked back to Mole. "I ain't got a particular game—I'm jus an all-round player. I go for the chicks, and they go for me. Then they is the supermarket I work for some days, when I got the time."

Mole's eyes flicked from Dwayne to Calvin,

and he nodded his head to Calvin and the two walked a little bit away.

Mole said, "You know that cat? He solid?"

Calvin said, "Yeah, I know him. He be together."

"He got no brother with the pigs or nothin?"

"Nah. He don't know no pigs."

Mole said, "We need a third. It good to have a cat don't live in the project."

"Dwayne solid on solid. You could ask him."

Mole got a soda out of the machine and strolled back toward Dwayne. "What you into tonight, man?"

"I ain't into nothin special." Dwayne didn't want to get maneuvered into a spot where he'd need to spend money, so he took his dime out of his pocket and spun it in the air. He joked, "Look like me and my dime goin to have a thin time tonight."

"Hang around, man, we could use you."

"Yeah? Like how?"

"Just hang loose, man, we show you. Calvin and me got us a little business. You ain't got to be livin on one thin dime. Right, Calvin?"

"Right on!" Calvin winked.

"They's a dude here I got to straighten out," Mole said. "I see you over to your place later."

"O.K., man. Me and Dwayne be together."

They fooled around the rec building and then went to Calvin's apartment, which was on the second floor of one of the project buildings. Mole turned up in a little while. Calvin said, "See, my momma work at the hospital nights, so we got the place to ourselves. This is our headquarters."

"Cool. My momma work at the hospital, too, but she work days. She on my butt all evening."

"You just tell her to switch to nights, man," Mole laughed. "What you got to eat here, Calvin?"

Dwayne watched Calvin get out some bologna and pickles, and he thought uneasily about his mother waiting for him for supper. The phone was sitting here. He could call. But she'd want to know where he was, and he couldn't see trying to make something up with Mole and Calvin listening. There'd be cracks about his calling Momma up, like a little boy.

He put his bologna and pickle between bread and sauntered around the apartment.

"What building we going to?" Calvin asked.

"Next to the end, down on Twelfth."

"Good. I don't like to work too near home. Cats get to know me."

"We take the top floors. They ain't so suspicious up there."

"Mink comin with the stuff?"

"What you think we working for?"

"What time?"

"Bout ten. We be through then."

"How many bags?"

"Many as we got the bread for."

Dwayne turned the radio dial to another station. His back was to them. He thought, Bags . . . horse, the real stuff. His palms turned cold and sweaty. He'd seen pushers on the street. Never inside. Never talked to one. Maybe there was still some way he could get out of this.

He turned around and got a grin onto his face. "What time you cats goin to yo office? I don't want to be too late—my old man bust me."

"Boy, you got to ed-u-cate your momma and daddy! Don't worry, man—we get you home ten, eleven o'clock. That ain't past your bedtime, is it?" Mole looked at him, and Calvin laughed.

"Nah," Dwayne heard himself say. "I got time." Now there was no way out.

chapter
eleven

WHEN IT WAS almost dark, they left Calvin's apartment. Dwayne looked up at the shoebox buildings. Lights shone in some windows. Others were dark, some were broken, and whole rows of ground-floor windows were boarded up with bright orange painted plywood. Living in those apartments must be like living in a shooting gallery. Some buildings were entirely empty, deserted, no more targets.

They turned into a building just as a project guard was coming out. Calvin nodded and murmured, "Hey, man." The guard walked on past. They got into the elevator and Mole pushed the button for the top floor. The elevators only stopped every third floor.

"Hey, you watch 'Surf Boys' last night?" Calvin said.

"Man, that cat hit the other cat with the surf board . . ."

Their voices were loud and chatty, and Dwayne realized the conversation was just for show, just to sound natural, in case anyone else got on the elevator.

They got off and walked down one flight. Mole took Dwayne by the arm and went one way, and Calvin went the other. Mole said, "You stay with me. Stay cool, man. You don't do nothing this time—Calvin doing the work."

They watched Calvin walk to the far end of the corridor. He rang the first doorbell. No answer. He went to the next, listened at the door, then moved on. He rang at the third. Someone inside called, "Who that?"

"Ma name is Jai-mes Bufor', ma'am. Ah huntin for ma gran'momma, and ah cain't tell which do' is which, ma'am." Dwayne grinned at Calvin's voice, which sounded straight out of the Deep South. The lady inside shouted something back, but she didn't open the door. Calvin moved two doors down.

Suddenly Mole bumped into Dwayne and started walking down the corridor. In a high-pitched nasal voice, he said, "She is one slick chick if I ever see one! Man, she got big legs, she got big—" Mole gestured, grinning back at Dwayne, and then looking over his head. "Scuse me, sir!" He nudged Dwayne aside and let an old man go past them. He went on talking loudly. "I sure am going to ring her number . . ."

As Mole talked, his eyes aimed like needles at the old man's back. When the man stopped at a door and took out his key, Calvin came up from the other side and started in: "Ah'm from Miss'-sippi, sah, and ah be huntin' for ma gran'-momma . . ."

Mole grabbed the old man from the back, one arm crooked around his face, and the other yanking his jacket down. Calvin's hands darted like cockroaches into the man's pockets, and then Mole hooked his foot around the old man's leg and dumped him on the floor. He didn't struggle, didn't move. Everything was silent.

Mole turned and the others followed him to the stairs. They ran down two flights of stairs, and then Mole sauntered along the hall, talking baseball. At the other end of the hall, when they knew no one was watching them, he said to Calvin, "What you get?"

"Twelve is all."

"You drop the wallet down the trash chute?"

"Sure, man."

Dwayne asked, "Ain't we going to get out of the building?" He was scared, and he looked it.

"Cool it, man. If that old cat call the guard, he be looking for us to run out of the building. Sides, we got work to do. Twelve bucks don't buy beans." He looked right at Dwayne. "Get yourself together, man. Your turn coming up."

"What you want me to do?"

"Me and Calvin stand lookouts, and you knock on . . ."

"I can't do that cornpatch talk—I can't pull that off!" Dwayne's voice went up and it wasn't steady.

Mole looked at him with that squinty grin that had no laughs it it. "O.K., boy—I got a line for you. You be scared, see?"

"Huh?"

"You is scared right now, but what I mean— you going to knock on the door, and you going to sound scared. You be this little dude with a high voice, and his momma—oh, she had a fainting spell, I guess. You gotta get help. You knocking on the door and yelling, 'Please, ma'am, come help ma momma!' "

Mole stopped and his face went flat, expressionless. His eyes fixed Dwayne and he grabbed hold of his shoulder. "You got it, man? Cause you better have it. You better not make no mistake!"

Dwayne's hands went into fists in his pockets, and his fingers pressed sweat against his palms. He nodded.

Mole went on: "Me and Calvin, we on the stairs either side. Anyone come, we yell out, 'O.K., Momma, I be home ten o'clock!' That the signal, see? You hear that, you go along with Calvin. If you get somebody to open the door, me or Calvin be with you, whoever be the nearest. Got it?" His eyes checked Calvin and lingered a little longer on Dwayne. Then Mole and Calvin left him.

Dwayne was alone in the middle of the hall. He thought, This ain't me, it must be some other cat. My momma didn have no boy like this. She just got that Dwayne—he be a good boy. In crazy flashes before his eyes, he saw his mother's wide mouth smiling, and then his father's eyes and high, shiny forehead, with the hair going gray.

Mole whistled a snatch of "Dixie," and Dwayne jerked around to look at him and got an icy look back. Mole pointed one jabbing finger. Dwayne went to the first door on the corridor. He listened and heard a babble of kids' voices and a TV going. That was no good—too many people. He wiped his hands on his jeans, saved for a moment.

He went to the second door. Silence. He knocked, knocked again, remembering he was supposed to sound frantic and scared. There was no answer. He went to the next door and knocked some more. Still no answer. He began to hope— maybe no one would open a door.

His knuckles rattled on the next door. From inside he could hear soft gospel music.

"Who that?" It was an old lady's voice, and the music was turned down.

Dwayne sucked in his breath and felt himself trembling. "Please, ma'am! Help me, please, ma'am! Ma momma done fall down! She layin' on the floor . . . you gotta come help me! Please, ma'am!"

"Wait a minute, boy!" He heard shuffling footsteps, then a snicking sound at the lock. Instantly, he heard Mole coming down the hall, still whistling "Dixie."

He was scared—it wasn't hard to make his voice convincing. "Oh, hurry, ma'am, please . . ." There, the door wiggled, started to open. Before there was even a crack, and before the old lady could put the chain on, Mole crashed past Dwayne and hit the door. The door flew open, and there was an awful thump.

"Get in! Shut the door!" Mole ordered.

They were inside the apartment, and suddenly there was silence. Dwayne turned, and his stomach flipped. She was lying on the floor, an old lady with a fuzz of white hair haloing her black face. She hadn't even had time to look frightened. She just lay there, her face nice and peaceful, except for one thing. Her false teeth half hung out of her mouth, and a dribble of pink saliva ran out of the corner of her mouth.

Mole was moving. He grabbed the old lady's purse off a table and emptied it on the floor beside Dwayne. "Go through it! Just get the money!" He whirled and started pulling out bureau drawers.

Dwayne turned away from the old lady, but a sick, yellow taste hung in his throat. He picked at the litter from the pocketbook. He didn't really want to touch it, but he opened the change purse and took out a dollar and some change.

Mole swooped back toward him, jerked the pocketbook from his hands. "She gotta have more than that!" He put his foot on the purse and yanked out the lining. Bills tumbled out.

"Get that! Look under the mattress and pillow!" Mole barked, and he disappeared into the closet and started throwing clothes and boxes out.

Dwayne looked under the bed pillow and moved the mattress a little. Mole came back and took the bills from the pocketbook and fanned them out in his hand quickly. He looked over at the limp old woman and winked. "That a good granny! I knowed you have somethin for me! How bout your Holy Bible, granny?" He seized it from the bedside table and shook it by the cover. A twenty-dollar bill floated out. Mole pocketed it and said, "You a real good granny!"

Dwayne stood helplessly in the middle of the room. He couldn't stop his eyes going back to the old lady. She still looked peaceful, except for those teeth, and the pink trickle which was bigger now. He looked away.

Calvin's voice sounded from the hall: "O.K., Momma, I'll be home ten o'clock."

Mole's hand reached out to the bedside radio and tuned the gospel singer up a little louder. Then the two of them stood motionless.

There was a knock on the door. "Hannah, you there?"

Dwayne held his breath.

"Hannah?" the woman's voice again.

A man said, "Likely she fell asleep already. Don't be waking her."

"She musta doze off and left her radio going. She do that," the woman said.

Dwayne heard the footsteps moving away and let out his breath. Mole turned the radio down and listened at the door. As soon as he heard the other door open and close, he beckoned to Dwayne. "Walk out nice and easy, see? Just be cool." He looked past Dwayne at the old lady and jeered, "Sweet dreams! You be cool, too, granny!"

He closed the door softly. As soon as they were in the stairwell, he started talking and laughing. "You know what that chick say to me? She say, Mole, you is the mellowest . . ."

Dwayne felt as if his whole body was stiff, battered and inflexible. He managed to bend his knees to get down the stairs, and to get out a "Yeah!" or "Man!" when Mole paused. All he could see in front of him was that black face with the white hair, and the teeth.

They got to Calvin's apartment, and Mole beat a tattoo on the door. Calvin opened and said, "How you do, man?"

"We do all right, man!" They went inside and closed the door, and Mole tossed the money on the table. Calvin put his twelve down and started dividing it all up. He looked at Mole and jerked his head briefly toward Dwayne. "What he get?"

Mole looked at Dwayne, looked at him as if he was a Ping-Pong ball. He said, "Ten." His eyes dared Dwayne to question it.

Calvin handed Dwayne the ten, and Dwayne's cold hand stuffed it down in his pocket. He heard himself say, "O.K., you cats. Seeya around."

"You goin, man? What your hurry?" Mole mocked. "Ain't you want a coupla bags—Mink be here any minute."

"I get it some other time. I gotta be goin."

Mole winked at Calvin. "That cat look like he seen a ghost! You b'lieve in ghos's, boy? Run long to Momma, now!" He laughed, that low, icy laugh. "And keep your mouth shut, or you be a real ghost!"

Dwayne didn't even care. He went home, blown along the dim streets like a shadow. He still had the yellow taste in the back of his mouth. He came to his own street and saw the light on his porch. The ball that was his stomach tightened. Vaguely, he noticed a strange car parked in front of the door.

He pulled open the door and stumbled inside. Three people stared at him. "There he is—praise the Lord!" said his mother.

"Boy, come here!" his father shouted.

The third was his grandmother, a little old lady with a black face and white hair. The yellow taste would not be swallowed again. Dwayne clapped his hand over his mouth and ran for the toilet.

He sat on the bathroom floor, panting, his forehead resting against the cool porcelain of the toilet. He sat there quite awhile. He began to overhear them talking outside.

"Boy be sick—that why he so late," his gran'-momma said.

"What he sick from, that what I want to know!" said his father.

His mother opened the bathroom door. "You all right now?" He nodded, kept his eyes closed.

"Where you been? What you eat to make you sick like that?"

Dwayne knew he couldn't speak. His stomach was still churning, and he clutched it and stumbled into his room. He plunged onto the bed and buried his face in the pillow. He felt his mother pulling off his tennis shoes, and she covered him with a blanket. The door closed. The dark lit up with faces, all kinds of faces, spinning crazily. Mole's face, his mother's, Melvita, his father's voice came roaring as through a tunnel, his gran'momma, and then with every spin of the wheel that other face, the one with the blob of teeth.

Dwayne groaned, jumped up, and made for the bathroom again. Nothing really came up, just the yellowness. He got back to bed and once in the night he felt someone pat him gently on the back. Sometime he must have slept, but when he woke up, the faces were still there. They came toward him and retreated, instead of spinning.

He heard his mother come in to see how he was, but he kept his eyes tight shut and breathed deeply. His stomach felt all right now, but how could he get up and talk to them? If he didn't have to talk about it, maybe the whole thing would go away, it wouldn't have happened.

"Git outa that bed, boy! Stand up here and look at me!"

It was his father, and there was no way to play sick anymore. Dwayne swung his feet around to the floor and stood up. His eyes met his father's for an instant, an instant only.

"Where you been last night?"

"Mmm . . ."

"Answer me! And look at me!"

Dwayne's eyes tracked across his father again and he mumbled. "Out with some kids."

"You gone got yourself drunk, that it?"

Dwayne was about to shake his head, and then he thought, That would do. That ain't so bad.

He nodded, not looking up, and was unprepared for the fast smack across the face, first right cheek, then left.

"You look at me, boy! What you do that for?"

Dwayne looked, said nothing.

"You just stupid, that right?"

Dwayne nodded.

"Say it!"

"Yessir, I just stupid."

"You get in any other trouble?"

Dwayne shook his head and prayed he wouldn't have to speak. His father stared at him, a full minute. He said, "You get in any trouble, you better tell me bout it now. I don't want to hear bout it from nobody else, hear?"

Dwayne stared at the floor, swayed a little. He couldn't tell his father. There were no words. Only those faces.

"Well, you in trouble with me, boy, that for sure! You be home five o'clock every evening, and you not going nowhere after that. Not for a month. You got me?"

"Yessir."

"Now you get washed up and dressed, and you

come out and don't give your momma or your gran'momma no more grief, y' hear?"

Dwayne went in the bathroom and shucked off his clothes and got under the shower. When he came out, he felt better. He balled up the dirty clothes and was about to stuff them in the laundry basket when he remembered. The money. As if something might bite him, he slid his hand into the pocket and pulled out the ten. He stood bare naked, and looked at it.

There was nothing he could do with it. No place to put it, no way to spend it without someone asking where it came from. Slowly, in sort of a daze, he stretched out his arm and dropped it in the toilet and flushed it away.

All gone, all over, he thought. He looked at himself in the mirror, but it was all still there. It would always be part of him.

Somehow he got through breakfast and lunch and the day. His mother had gone to work, and his father stayed outside working on his car. His gran'momma clucked over him, made him a soft boiled egg and dry toast for breakfast for his stomach, and asked him about school and baseball and Melvita. She thought his father had been hard on him, so she tried to be extra nice. The nicer she was, the worse he felt.

She asked what he wanted her to cook for supper. "I dunno!" he answered irritably. "I be all right—don't keep askin me what I want!"

She looked hurt, and he felt ashamed. He turned on the TV and stared through the screen.

131

I ain't never goin to be able to tell anyone, he thought. No one know how evil I be. I ain't never goin to that project again. I can't look at that Mole, Calvin neither.

On the evening news that night, the announcer said an elderly woman from the Darst-Webbe Project had been taken to the hospital, after burglars broke into her apartment and knocked her down. Dwayne realized suddenly that he heard news like that on the TV every day, and he never listened to it. His mother and father were hardly listening now.

Only his gran'momma said, "Poor soul! Maybe she don't have nothing worth taking, anyway. Who would do a thing like that?"

No one looked at Dwayne.

chapter
twelve

BRIAN'S TEACHERS, who thought he never heard a word in class, would have been surprised at how lost he felt after school let out. School was safe. Teacher and students had accepted him as a zero at a desk, and no one bothered him much.

No one bothered him at home, actually. Eve and Andy were out, and his mother sat with her knitting and her radio. But if he stayed home, little by little the sound of her radio and the feeling of her being there made him edgy. She would take the radio with her, if she went in the kitchen or up to her bedroom. The sound of it moving about the house, coming closer or moving away, got to him. He went out.

He stayed on the bigger, more open streets, where there were plenty of people. One skinny kid alone on the street, like a lame dog or a sick cat, could become the target for a bored bunch of kids. Brian looked ahead, down every block. He saw Dwayne in the distance a few times, with a bunch of other boys, swinging their bats and gloves, but he didn't think of joining them. Sometimes he lay on the grass in the park near Melvita and Martha, when they were baby-sitting. After Martha went to Illinois, he spent most of his time in Maisie's yard with Slanty.

Martha's cousin lived on a farm in Illinois. There was a garden full of vegetables and a yard full of little squealing pigs. Martha and Katie fed carrots to the pigs and laughed because the two biggest pigs tried to get all the carrots. They bit the little ones and made them squeal. Martha found it was easier not to eat so much herself. There was no place you could walk to for pizzas or ice cream. She stopped eating potatoes and filled up on all the farm vegetables, and she lost ten pounds.

Still, after a while, she was ready to come back to St. Louis. It might be dusty and clattery and crowded, but it was home and she missed her family.

The first morning after she was back, she said,

"C'mon, Katie, we go in the park. They got grass there, just like Illinois."

"No pigs," Katie said.

"Maybe we see Melvita and Precious—she be your friend."

"She bite me. She mean, like that big pig!"

Martha laughed. "Don't tell her that—she bite you for sure!" In the park she found Melvita and flopped down on the bench beside her. "Hey, girl, we is back! What happenin?"

"Same ole, same ole. Get up, clean up, chase this mean ole Precious. C'wan, Precious, you and Katie go play on the bars, and you play nice, y' hear?"

"You been anywhere?" Martha asked.

"Yeah, Dwayne's daddy drove us out to Six Flags, way out there in the country, you oughta see! We see them big houses with yards like a park, and we go on rides and everything. Dwayne throwin money round like he had a pocketful."

"He get him a job?"

"Not yet. He been tryin. Maybe he be at Happy's tonight. You comin?"

"I reckon. Where else?"

That Sunday at Happy's Melvita looked for Dwayne. His pals were there, Terry and Willie. "Where that Dwayne?" Melvita asked. "You see him today?"

"I ain't see him since Friday. That was enough! He one hardhead boy!"

"You have a fight?"

"We don't have no fight. We just tell him, when he be tagged out, he is out, just like anybody else!" Terry said. "Right, he ain't the catbird all the time," Willie said.

"I seen him walkin long the street, yesterday afternoon. Walkin down toward the project," Willie said.

"He mess with those cats, he find out. They ain't no good!"

Willie grinned at Melvita. "Maybe Dwayne find himself a fine chick down there!"

"Huh! He don't go with no project chick! He do, I get myself a new man!"

"How bout me?" Willie tried to take her arm. She shook him off. "I say a man, boy!"

She hung around with Martha and Sharon and a bunch of the others. They laughed and danced and drank their sodas, like always, but Melvita didn't feel good. She kept looking down the street, watching for Dwayne. The way they were, they didn't exactly make a date to meet at Happy's, they just each knew the other would be there. Where else could he have gone last night? Where was he tonight?

She and Martha went to Happy's the next night, and the night after that, and Dwayne wasn't there. Melvita stood sullen-faced and silent for a while, and the other kids steered away from her. Then, one night, she jumped in and started dancing and shouting louder and faster than any of them.

The next few nights her mother was out and she had to stay at home. She slapped the children's dinner on the table with none of her usual chatter, and she put them to bed early, so that she could sit out on the porch by herself, alone and gloomy. What could have happened? If he was on a punishment, or gone visiting, he could call, couldn't he? She thought of telephoning herself, but she just let herself get mad. He want to go off without sayin nothin, he can! I ain't goin beg him.

The next night she was at Happy's, and she heard Willie say, "He ain't never stay mad this long before." Terry said, "We need him for the game next week."

"You been by his house?" Willie said.

"I been by, and he lyin on the hammock readin a comic, and I say, 'Hey, Dwayne, what goin on?' And he say, 'Hey,' so low I can't hardly hear him, and he just go on readin his comic."

"He be one hardhead boy!" Willie said.

Melvita listened, and the words seemed to spin around inside her head, and then she felt her pulse pounding and her fists clenching up. So that's what! He just be lyin round home, doin nothin!

Suddenly she heard herself speaking in a harsh, jaunty tone. "Don't worry yoself bout that Dwayne! I hear he be goin to Kansas City— things too slow for him round here!"

Terry and Willie stared at her. "Yeah? Where you hear that, girl?"

"Oh, he call me on the telephone," she lied. "Guess he just ain't got time to call all of you cats!"

She swaggered away, glad to hit out at some-one, even if it was only Terry and Willie. She was sick of them anyway. She found Martha down toward the corner, where the high-school kids hung out. They were listening to this big cat, James. He was sitting on the fender of a parked car and talking. He wanted them to go on strike to change the name of the high school from McKinley High to Medgar Evers High.

"How bout Angela Davis High?" a tall girl with a big Afro shouted.

James spoke quietly. "They ain't goin do that when she been in jail."

"So we go on strike!"

Melvita stood next to Martha. She said, "I like that James. I like the way he look."

Melvita looked at him and at the rest of the group. "He look too serious for me. I like a cat to fun around with. That one over there, singin his-self a song. I goin to get him to sing one for me."

Martha laughed, but in a couple of minutes Melvita was over there with the boy she'd pointed to, and they were laughing and singing together. Martha went back to listening to James. He had a way of talking very low, so that the others had to be quiet and gather in close to listen. Martha moved in with them. The one who wanted Angela Davis High interrupted a few times, and then she and some others looked disgusted and walked away. James watched them go for a mo-ment, then went on talking. Martha recognized a boy who lived near her. He raised his hand

and said, "Hey, girl," and she said, "Hey, Roy," and she felt as if she was part of the group.

After a while, kids drifted away in twos and threes. Melvita brought over the boy she'd found. "This here is Anthony. Anthony, that my friend, Martha. How bout you all stop arguin and start singin?"

Anthony looked at Martha and rolled his eyes a little. "Martha, I bet you got one fine big voice!"

"To go with the rest of me, you mean? You ain't fool me—I see them eyeballs spinnin!"

Anthony laughed easily. "Me, I like a comfortable woman. Come on, let me hear you." He put one arm around Melvita and started snapping the fingers of his other hand, bending and straightening, tapping his feet. "James, boy—hit it!" he begged.

"I sing like a lead balloon, you know it," James said.

"Roy, give us a bass!" Anthony crooned. Roy joined in and then Martha. She had a feeling James was watching her and she sang out, but she stood still, not stamping and shaking the way she sometimes did.

Above them a window banged up and a strident voice yelled, "Quiet down there!"

Anthony shook his head sadly. "Got no soul, no soul at all! C'mon, give her the chorus!" When they ended he said, "Les go someplace else. Can't stand those womens shoutin at me."

James said, "I told some cats over to Northside I be meetin them. You comin?"

"O.K.," Anthony said. "How bout you chicks?"

Martha and Melvita looked at each other. They weren't sure. They weren't quite ready to go anywhere. Melvita said, "My momma want me to come home. Baby been sick, and she ain't got much sleep."

Martha said, "My momma, she worry if I don't come home. Some other night, I tell her I be late."

"You be here tomorrow night, hey, girl?" Anthony said.

"Sure, where else," Melvita said.

Martha just barely caught James's eyes. He raised his hand. "Night."

"Night," she said.

Martha and Melvita sat in the park the next morning. For a while neither of them said much, but they both knew they were thinking about the same thing.

Finally Martha said, "Where that ole Dwayne? I ain't see him since I come back." She knew something was wrong, but Melvita had avoided talking about it.

"I dunno."

"Maybe he goin visiting someplace."

Melvita reared up. "He ain't goin visiting! He lyin on his backside on the hammock, and he can lie there till he rot! Ain't nothin to do with me!"

"He might of got on a punishment, can't go out."

"He could call."

"Yeah, I reckon. Still, maybe somethin really bad happen, like someone sick or dead."

"Puh! He could phone."

"Still, I was you, I'd call, at least once."

Melvita snapped, "You ain't me, and I ain't callin!" She stared out across the park, letting the anger fill her up again. Precious pushed Katie out of the swing, and Melvita jumped up and spanked vigorously. "Wait'll you get to school—teacher goin whup you good!" she threatened. She felt better after letting off a little steam.

"Hey, Martha, you got a boy friend? You ain't going with that Brian, is you?"

"I ain't going with him, I just be with him sometimes. I ain't see him since I get back from Illinois. Must be, he moonin round with that ole dog."

Melvita said, "I think that Anthony cute. Him and James. He sort of serious, but he cute, too. You want to go someplace with them some night?"

There it was, the question they'd both been working around toward.

Martha said, "James look real nice. I like the way he sound, but I ain't even talk to him yet."

"I see him lookin at you last night. He was really lookin, girl!"

"Yeah?"

"Anyhow, we ain't makin no lifetime commitment! We just goin someplace beside ole Happy Jack."

Martha said, "My momma get mad if I go in bars."

"Anthony say he know some spots where they be singin and dancin. He don't say they's bars."

"James, he go to a lot of meetins. I don't mind. He sound like he really mean what he say."

"Anyway, it be Saturday night," Melvita said. "You tell your momma you goin be little late. Then if we want to go someplace, we could."

They got to Happy's that night and went straight down to the corner. James and Anthony were there with some others.

"Hey, Melvita!" Anthony said. "What the word?"

"Cele-bration, how bout that?"

"What celebration?"

"I don't know. Let's have one!"

"You want to celebrate with a pizza and a soda?"

"That all right with me."

James moved along toward Martha and leaned against the fence. "I hear you singin last night, but I don't even know your name."

"You be the only one," Martha laughed. "Everybody know fat Martha!"

"I ain't live here long," James said. "You like a pizza, Martha?"

"I love pizza, but I ain't goin to have one, thank you."

James looked at her directly. "You don't want to get fat, hunh?"

"I don't want to *be* fat, and that what I be, you know it!"

James shrugged, but he didn't start joking the way most people did. He said, "Take it easy, girl. Ain't no one goin tell you how to run your own body. You got a right to eat, or not to eat. How bout a soda?"

"That be nice."

He came back with two sodas, and he said, "Where you at, Martha?"

"You mean school? Clinton, dumb ole Clinton."

He smiled. "Where else?"

Martha said slowly, "Well, I don't know. I didn't really think yet."

"Yeah, nobody like to think much. It tire the body and tire the mind."

"I hear you talkin to the kids a lot. I wish I goin to high school this year. I be in that ole Clinton eight long years."

"We do a few little things in school. Like we tryin to change the name. Big things, we can't do much bout." James nodded his head toward the next corner. "Like the junkie standin right there, big as life; any kid can buy it."

"Kids must be crazy, doin that," Martha said.

James shook his head. "They ain't crazy, they just people. The stuff be there, it make 'em feel good, so they take it. Just as easy as for you to have you a piece of pizza."

"Why can't the po-lice get them junkies?"

"Good question. But the answer be a long way off."

"What be a long way off?" Anthony broke in. "Cause I been here long nough. Me and Melvita ready for a change of scene! Right, girl?"

"Right."

They sauntered down the street, and James and Martha fell in behind them. Nobody really said where they were going. Now that she'd talked to James, Martha wasn't worried—he didn't act wild, like some of them. That night, they just walked across the railroad tracks over to the big post office, where the fountains were. They put their feet in the water and watched the moon and the stars and the airplanes over the Arch.

"It could be a pretty city, someday," James said. He and Martha leaned back to back, comfortably, and their hands played together in the water.

Melvita and Anthony listened to his little radio and talked. Melvita looked at them reflected in the water, and for one instant Melvita thought, What if that be Dwayne? She shook her head, felt the tight yarn bow pulling against her scalp, and pulled it off. She shook her hair out loose. She put Dwayne out of her head, too.

By the end of July, everyone at Happy's knew those four were together. Kids from Clinton looked at Martha and Melvita and sniffed, Huh, they think they so big! The high-school bunch shrugged and thought, Aw, that be jus for summer—that ain't nothin serious.

chapter
thirteen

BRIAN HEARD the announcer on television say it was the first day of August. It seemed to him a long time since school let out. Every day was about the same, and every day nothing happened. He'd been around to Martha's house twice, but she wasn't there. Her mother said, "She might be over to Melvita's. You know where that is, Brian?"

"Yes, ma'am," said Brian, but he didn't go. Doing nothing got to be a habit, and it was easy to lie under the bush with Slanty. Sometimes old Maisie called the dog and he stayed outside by himself. One day when it was cooler, he set off, just wanting to walk somewhere.

He came to the corner of Caroline Street and he remembered, that was Dwayne's street. He paused. Probably Dwayne was off playing ball. Still, maybe he wasn't. Maybe he was doing some more work on the house—it'd be a good day for working.

He walked down the street and right past the house, not recognizing it all painted. Then he heard an old lady on the porch say, "Something be on Dwayne's mind, for sure. He don't act right."

"Mmm, he be that age." That was Dwayne's mother. "I used to worry cause he be out all the time, now I worry cause he stay home."

"Keepin a young boy home evenins for a whole month, that be hard on him."

"His daddy know what he doing."

The screen door slammed. "Hello, Dwayne, honey," the old lady said.

Brian paused and looked back. That was it, all right. That was the porch he'd scraped.

"Hey, Dwayne!" Brian called.

Dwayne looked up, blank for an instant, then grinned. "Hey, Brian!"

His mother turned. "Why, hello, Brian. We didn't see you for a while."

Brian smiled. "I walked right past the house. I didn't recognize it, all painted."

"Ain't it pretty? Dwayne do a real good job. Brian, this here is Dwayne's gran'momma."

"Afternoon, ma'am."

"I goin to make some cookies in a little while," the grandmother said. "You come round."

"Where you goin, Brian?" Dwayne asked.

"No place special."

"Want to see if they got a movie up at the library?"

"O.K."

They walked up the street toward Jefferson Avenue. "What you been doin, besides paint the house?" Brian said.

"Not much. Used to play ball some, but I got mad at them dumbheads."

Brian was sort of pleased at that, and he didn't ask any questions. He said, "My old brother plays ball a lot, but I never got onto it. I'd forgotten about the movies at the library—how often they have 'em in summer?"

"Two, three times. They goin to have *Frankenstein*."

"Yeah?"

They crossed Jefferson Avenue. Dwayne sighed and relaxed. If he was out of the house, he spent most of his time up this way now, because he wasn't so likely to see kids he knew. After that night in the project with Calvin and Mole, he felt . . . well, he'd never felt like that before, so he didn't know how he felt. He didn't want to talk to anyone.

He was afraid of meeting Mole or Calvin on the street, and the fear itself unnerved him. He'd never been afraid of a kid, never skulked around to avoid someone. He always thought he owned the street.

He didn't want to talk to Terry and Willie either. Other times, when he'd had fights with the kids, they'd always made it up a day or two later. Now weeks had gone by and he'd have to make up some big story, why he hadn't been around, why he didn't even speak to Terry that time at the house. He didn't feel like making up big stories.

But the worst was Melvita. Being ashamed to tell your parents something, or being on the outs with some of the kids playing ball—that could happen. Before, he'd never felt ashamed to tell Melvita something. He'd always been able to tell her funny stories or invent alibis, when they both knew it was just talk. He'd never had to tell her a down-and-out lie.

That was what it came to now. In his own mind, Dwayne didn't see how any mere excuse could cover what he'd done down at the project, so there was no excuse to tell Melvita why he hadn't met her that Saturday night, or Sunday night, or any night. It would have to be a big, foolproof lie. Or nothing. Days went by, and it was still nothing. Lying on his bed, he would invent opening phrases. "Hey, Melvita, you ain't goin believe what happen . . ." or, "Melvita, listen, girl, you got to trust me . . ." He would wait for a time when no one was near the phone to overhear him, but then his hand would not pick it up. There was nothing he could say. As he hesitated near the phone, his mother or grandmother would come in, and Dwayne would shrink back into his room, fling himself on the bed and prop a comic in front of his face.

He couldn't stand the way they kept looking at him. Questioning, anxious, and . . . sweet. Dwayne clenched his teeth. *They don't be sweet if they know. They goin to hate me. I got to get outa this house.*

As Dwayne and Brian crossed Jefferson now, Brian remembered that was where he'd first seen Slanty. He said, "Hey, I didn't tell you—I found my dog."

"Yeah? Where you find him?"

"You know the old lady in the little house on the park? One they call crazy Maisie? He stays in her yard."

Dwayne tightened up. He knew Maisie's yard well enough—it backed on Melvita's. They cut through there often.

"You wanta come see him, maybe? After we seen the movie?"

"Nah, man. Dog just be a dog. You seen one, you seen 'em all."

"Slanty's different . . ."

"C'mon, le's see what movie they goin to have!"

It turned out there was no movie that day. "You know how to play checkers?" Dwayne asked.

"Unh-unh."

"I show you how. Man, I be the checker champ of Barr Branch Library!" Dwayne had to be best at something.

He started showing Brian how to play, and for

the first few games, Dwayne won before Brian had hardly got started. Then Brian started concentrating, trying to figure the moves out ahead. He got better.

"Ain't it make you mad, I beat you all the time?" Dwayne said, beginning to get bored with the game.

"Why would I get mad? Go ahead—your move."

Dwayne moved a man carelessly. Brian grinned and jumped two men. "Man! What you think you doin?"

"I did it! Your move."

Dwayne won again, but it was getting harder. They'd gotten to a game that almost looked like a stalemate, when it was library closing time. Dwayne looked at Brian and said, "You really learn that game fast! Most of the dudes I play with, I beat 'em coupla times and they won't play no more."

Brian laughed excitedly. "I might beat you someday!"

"Huh! You ain't goin to beat me!" Dwayne said out of habit.

They walked to Dwayne's house. His grandmother was sitting outside, and there was a plate of cookies. She offered it to Brian, and said, "Dwayne, honey, maybe you oughta save yours for dessert. Dinner be ready in a minute."

Dwayne screwed up his face in mock agony. "Aw, that be no fair! He got some . . ." When he saw he'd taken his grandmother in, he started laughing.

She smiled. "Sure good to hear you happy, boy. First time I really hear you laugh." Dwayne remembered, and stopped. She said, "You come again, Brian, hear? I keep the cookies ready."

"Thank you, ma'am," he said. "Bye."

chapter
fourteen

IN THE MORNINGS now Brian went to feed Slanty, and he lay under the bush with him in that green cave and looked at comics or went back to sleep. In the afternoons, he went to see Dwayne.

They started exploring the part of the city that lay west and north of their neighborhood. They'd never gone that way much before. One day, they walked a couple of miles, as far as Gaslight Square. Dwayne recognized the old glass lanterns with the little gaslight inside. "Yeah, I seen them before! My daddy drove me round here once. There used to be all these fancy restaurants, and then they get to be all these hippies and junkies, and everyone get mugged and beat up. This a bad part of town, man!"

It was somewhat deserted now. The restaurants had closed up and a good many houses were boarded up. "It looks about like our part of town," Brian said.

"Yeah, but they got big buildings up here, too. You see that big church back there, took up the whole block? Man, they must got a lotta money! That be why the junkies and the bad cats move in, they smell money."

Momentarily, he thought of Mole, and the junkie he hadn't waited to see down in the project. Ain't a whole lot of money down there, he thought. Just ordinary folks, ole ladies. . . . He put the picture out of his mind.

They walked past an old house, and they could hear music from a radio inside. It didn't sound like the same music you usually hear on the street. Dwayne listened. "Music teacher in school play that kinda stuff," he said.

A sign over the door said WDNA—Free Radio. Brian said, "It ain't just somebody's radio; the sign says it's a radio station."

"Aw, couldn't be no radio station! They big. This just an old house, with a bunch of dudes and chicks hangin round."

A group was sitting on the steps and lounging on the porch. The girls had long hair and some of them wore shorts and some long skirts, and the boys had on jeans and undershirts or no shirts. Dwayne looked at them doubtfully. All of them were white. Then two black guys came out of the building and sat down on the steps, too.

Without thinking, Brian spoke up. "How come that music sounds different?"

A girl laughed. "Different from what?"

"Sound like jive stuff to me," Dwayne said stubbornly.

A kid with a curly red beard said, "Man, you're talking about the 'Rites of Spring,' by Mr. Igor Stravinsky, a traveler from a distant land. Go ahead, you could dance!"

"Can't dance with that!"

"What's that sign mean?" Brian said. "Is this really a radio station?"

"Come on in, I'll show you," the boy with the beard said. Brian started up the walk and Dwayne followed, walking sort of alert and uneasy. You couldn't tell about cats like these. His eye caught the eye of one of the black guys. The man raised one hand slightly. "Hey, man," he said. "Hey, man," Dwayne answered. Inside, the room was dark after the sunny street, and they walked through it to a brightly lit glassed-in booth at the far end. There were several record turntables and a man and a girl with earphones on. The record finished, and they could see the man changing it, and then he started talking and his voice came out all around them.

"Man!" Dwayne breathed. "It really do be a radio station!"

Another record went on, several lights inside the control room blinked on and off, and the red-bearded guy stuck his head in the door. When he talked to the people inside, his voice didn't come out of the speakers. He came back to Brian and Dwayne. "O.K., you want to come inside? My name's Nat. What's yours?"

There was hardly space inside the little control room for them all. The man with earphones took them off and handed them to Nat. "Go ahead, you be announcer."

The girl took off her headset and handed it to Brian. "You want to talk?" she asked, and Brian shrank.

"I can talk!" Dwayne said. "What you want me to say?"

Nat showed them the different switches and lights in the room, and when the record finished, he spoke into his mouthpiece. "We got a visitor named Dwayne at the station here. How d'you like the music we've been playing, Dwayne?"

Dwayne heard him through his earphones, and he laughed. He said, "That the kind of jive stuff the music teacher play at school."

"Yeah? Where you go to school, Dwayne?"

"Clinton."

"How's that, a pretty good school?"

"Nah, man, it be a drag. I don't dig school."

"How about you, Brian?"

Nat held a mike in front of Brian, and Brian said, "Well, it's all right. It's a place to go."

"What kind of music you like, Dwayne?" Nat asked.

"Soul music. Anything what got some soul. The Black Eyes, Tom Brown, lotta different cats."

One of the black guys looked inside the control room and beckoned to Dwayne. "Hey, you don't dig ole Clinton, huh? Me neither, I used to go there."

"How you hear me?" Dwayne asked.

"Everyone hear you. You on the air, all over St. Louis."

"Yeah! For real? Wait'll I tell the cats at school." Dwayne said it, and then he remembered he wasn't talking to them, and he couldn't tell Melvita either.

"We got a lot of records here," the other man said. "You want to pick one?"

Dwayne found a record he knew, and they showed him how to put it on the turntable. He spoke into the headset again. "O.K., folks, get ready —here come the real soul music!"

He and Brian went out of the control room after a bit, and Nat took them around the rest of the house. There was a kitchen upstairs and a girl cutting up vegetables. "Hey, Shanks, what's for lunch?" Nat said.

Dwayne looked at her and thought, How can a skinny ole girl like that cook food? She don't eat.

"Turnip salad." Nat made a face. "Turnips is what's good and cheap down at Soulard right now," Shanks said. "They're nice little ones—I got good tomatoes and peppers, too."

"I go to Soulard," Brian said. "I've got a friend there, this farmer from Arkansas. He gives me stuff."

"Yeah? You show me which one—I'll see you there some Saturday. You want some lunch now?"

"I dunno bout them turnips," Dwayne muttered. "My momma cook 'em and they be mushy."

"That's cooked," she said. "These are raw."

So they ate. They thought the salad tasted funny, but it was pretty good, and they liked listening to the kids talk and the radio play. There was a speaker in every room.

The radio station got to be one more place they went sometimes, only it was a pretty long walk. But Brian couldn't get Dwayne to go with him to Soulard. The next Saturday that Brian went there, he saw the skinny girl from the radio station and rode back with her.

Instead of going with Brian, Dwayne went to the library. He didn't like the movie, and there was no one to play checkers with. Bored, he riffled through some magazines. He looked around the room and saw one set of shelves marked The Black Experience. He walked over and picked out the first book that caught his eye —it had a bold black and white cover.

He opened the book and started reading, not even bothering to check the title, and right away on the first page there was this boy trying to kill a rat, and his mother and sister yelling, and the boy was cussing and he killed the rat.

Dwayne walked to the nearest chair, still reading. He didn't know they put things like that in books, bad words and rats, and a boy talking just the way he talked himself, not book language at all. He read slowly and it took him awhile to finish the first chapter. He closed the book and looked at the title, *Native Son*.

"He some son!" Dwayne said and started the next chapter. The boy's name was Bigger, and Dwayne liked that. Bigger and some other fellows were getting ready to rob a candy store, and they were scared. Just then the librarian, a young black man, came up and told him it was closing time.

Dwayne looked up at him. "Man, I can't quit now! This dude just about to rob a store, or he might get killed his own self!"

The librarian turned the book over to see the title. He laughed, "Aw, he ain't going to get killed right off! Why don't you take it home?"

"Can I?"

"You got a card?"

"Unh-unh. Ain't never needed one before."

The librarian grinned again. "Man, you sure needing one now—you can't forget about Bigger. Come over here."

He showed Dwayne how to fill out the application and said he could take the book home on a temporary card. Dwayne read it when he was alone in bed that night, because he was afraid his mother would pick it up and see the bad words. Monday he went back to the library with the book—he liked reading it there, and there were some things maybe he was going to want to ask the librarian.

The same librarian wasn't there for a couple of days, so Dwayne just read. He read about Bigger robbing the candy store, and then Bigger went to work for this white family, and they were really nice to him, but Dwayne kept thinking, Something spooky about them people, how come they act like they do? He remembered the big houses he'd seen outside St. Louis and he wondered, How the people in them houses act, what they really like? They ghosts, like in Bigger's book?

He stopped reading for a bit and stared out the window, and suddenly it was there again, the picture of that nice old face with the white hair, and the crooked mess of false teeth hanging out. But it was a black face looking at him and asking, Why? Dwayne shut his eyes and put his head down on the table.

"Man, you ain't falling asleep over that book, are you?"

Dwayne jerked up. The black librarian was back.

"I ain't sleepin." Dwayne paused, then suddenly blurted: "How come black people all the time beatin up on other black people?"

The librarian looked puzzled. "That Bigger, that's a white family he's working for . . ."

"Unh . . . yeah, I don't mean that. I mean like, on the TV, when they show some ole black lady get mugged, it usually be some black cat what did it."

"Unh . . . that. Yeah." The librarian looked at Dwayne and it seemed as if he looked right through him. Then he said softly, "That something to think about, man. You dig on it."

Dwayne picked up the book. "I got to find out bout these things."

"You look in the books, and you look round

you, and you look inside your own head, too. You dig on it."

The librarian walked away, and Dwayne thought, Inside my own head? Do he know what I done? Nah, he couldn't. He don't know I rob that old lady. He ain't there.

When the library closed that afternoon, he walked out on the street and stood a moment, staring around, but still half lost inside his book. He walked toward home, and he noticed that all the people on the street around him were black. The people in that project where the old lady lived, they were all black. How come no white people there? he thought.

He knew the answer to that. The white people moved out where there were better houses, and it was a safer neighborhood. He always heard that phrase "safe neighborhood." It was always someplace else, not where he lived. He shook his head, Don't make no sense. My momma want to live where it safe. So do that ole lady. So why don't they move?

He looked up, and his heart thumped. He forgot all about those questions because there was Melvita walking along the street ahead of him. She was with Martha. He felt his pulse pounding with pleasure and with fear that she would be sore at him. Maybe she wouldn't pick a fight in front of Martha. Anyway, he wouldn't stop to think.

"Hey, Melvita! Hey, wait up a minute!"

She paused and looked back at him. "Wait up for what?" She tossed her head defiantly, and went on walking.

"Listen, Melvita—I got to talk to you!"

"Ain't nothin to talk about."

"About not getting to Happy's—see, I got to explain . . ."

Melvita stopped, turned, glared right at him. "Boy, you ain't got to explain bout somethin what happen two-three weeks ago! You just do what you want with your own self! Make no difference to me."

"Aw, listen . . ."

"Go where you want to go, and I go where I want to go! Me and Martha got our own plans, right, Martha?"

"Right!" Martha laughed.

The laugh stung Dwayne. "Listen, you goin with some other dude?"

"None of your business, boy. You go long with them chicks down in the project, tell them bout it. My man ain't none of your business!"

"I kill him!"

"Ha! He cut you down like a grasscutter cutting grass! Little boys don't mess with him!"

"You think you so great! I suppose you go in the alley with any old jive cat that look at you . . ."

"Shut yo evil mouth, boy! I don't even hear you!" Melvita turned and walked away. Dwayne stood there. Strings of insults ran through his head, but he knew they were useless. He would never say them. Worst of all, in the back of his head, he knew he was wrong. He was the one who hadn't showed up, and hadn't called. Now she was gone.

chapter
fifteen

BRIAN HADN'T SEEN Martha since she'd
come back from Illinois. He'd been busy exploring with Dwayne. One Sunday morning, Brian
was leaning on old Maisie's fence talking to the
dog when Melvita came by, cutting through the
backyards from her house.

"Boy, you better watch out!" she called. "Don't
you know ole Maisie be's a witch? She put her
evil eye on you, you be finished!"

"Aw, she ain't no witch—she just gets things
mixed up. Like she always calls me Bobby."

"You mean you been talkin to her?"

"Sure, I talk to her anytime she comes outside.

See, she's got this whole bunch of people, she thinks they're really alive. There's James and Esther and Lydia, and Bobby—that's me. She tells me they're doing this or that, and then she always ends up, 'They've gone away. Everyone's gone away, they don't come anymore.' So I come, and she knows me, sort of."

"Well, I declare!" Melvita stared at him. "Boy, you really talkin today!" She looked over at the window where Maisie's curtain twitched, and Melvita laughed. "Take ole Maisie to find out. That tickle me—take one to know one! What you do, jus come over here and talk to her?"

"I come to see my dog. Old Maisie keeps him for me." Slanty was sitting under his bush, his head cocked suspiciously at Melvita.

She looked at him and made a face. "I hate dogs!"

"You can't hate a dog!" Brian was shocked.

"I sure can! Boy, you see that?" Melvita pointed to one strong knee and showed him a long white scar. "See that? Dog do that."

"I suppose some dogs get mean. People kick 'em or something."

"I was just a little bitty thing, bout six year old. My momma send me to the store with five dollars scrunch up in my hand, and I be scared to death I lose it and she goin whup me. An I see this mean ole big doberman dog an I run an I fell down and cut my leg open on a piece of glass . . ."

"Oh, he didn't bite you."

"Might jus as well! That dog make me cut my leg open. They take me to the hospital, and all these white people with white masks and white nightgowns be bendin over me and I think I dead, for sure. Then they go jab, stitch, jab, stitch—I be alive all right, and they sewin me up like an ole rag. Man, that hurt! I lose my five dollars, too. Now you know why I hate dogs!"

"My dog ain't mean . . ."

"You see this?" Melvita held out an arm with a smaller scar on it. "Dog do that, too. He try to steal my tennis shoes off the porch, an I hit him with a stick and try an grab my shoe back, and he bite me! An up here on my chin, puppy bite me. I ain't even hit him, I just playing. They jus evil, dogs is!"

"Slanty was running along the street when I found him. He was scared and hungry. He was . . . well, sort of a dropout. You know, just living on the street. So now he lives here with Maisie, and I come feed him."

"You sure have change, boy. You know who was talkin bout you, few days ago?"

"Huh?"

"Martha, that who. She wonderin if you goin away."

"She went away."

"Aw, she been back, coupla weeks now! Where you been?"

"I been hanging around with this kid, Dwayne. He's in school—I guess you know him."

Melvita tossed her head. "I guess he one of them hardhead boys always hollerin and fightin. I don't hang round with them. I tell Martha I see you, though."

Brian didn't wait for that; he walked down to Martha's house himself. Katie was out front, and he called, "Hey, Katie, where's Martha?"

"She inside. Where you been? You been away?"

"Unh-unh."

"I been away. I been on my farm and we got pigs. You ever see a pig?"

"Not close, just from a bus."

"I be close! I feed 'em carrots."

Brian walked past her and knocked at the door. A man was standing just inside and he looked at Brian doubtfully.

"Is Martha there?" he said.

"Martha!"

She came from the kitchen and saw Brian. "Brian! Boy, I thought you done disappear from the face of the earth. Brian, this my father."

Her father grinned. "Mornin, Brian, come in. I was holdin back cause I thought you be sellin somethin!"

Martha came outside. "Where you been hidin, boy?"

"I been around. You know that kid, Dwayne. He's at school."

"Yeah, and ain't nobody see him in a coupla weeks, either! What the two of you doin?"

"We just sort of go places. We went up to Gaslight Square, and there's this radio station with a lot of kids. Then we go to the library . . ."

"Yeah, I seed Dwayne up that way yesterday . . ." Martha puzzled over it. Dwayne never hung around with any little old scared kid like Brian before, and he never read books before.

"Where you find Dwayne?" she said.

"Down to his house. See, I helped him scrape paint on his house—that was awhile ago."

"How yo momma doin? She better now?"

"She's all right I guess. She ain't drinking."

"That be good! See, she get better in the hospital."

"Yeah."

"What yo sister doin?"

"She got a good job, down at Ralston. She's sort of a secretary there."

"Mmm, that what I like! Next year, I goin get me a job there. After I take typing in school."

"I guess Eve's pretty smart."

"Boy, you gettin yo smarts, too! You quit fightin with her?"

"Yeah, we get along all right. We got along good when my mom was in the hospital. Even Andy—I got along with him then. He's sort of growing up."

"Listen to you, gran'pa!" she teased.

"How bout me? You think I look different?"

He looked at her, puzzled. "Mmm, I don't know."

"I got a boy friend," she said. "He be real serious, and he go to the high school."

"Yeah?"

"You come round again, Brian. I been missin you. I gotta go help Momma now, fore we go to church. I see you."

"O.K. Seeya."

Brian went around to find Dwayne, but Dwayne was in a sour mood and didn't want to stop reading his book. He pushed over a stack of old comics so Brian looked at them for a while. They ate lunch, and Dwayne's grandmother talked a lot and kept trying to get Dwayne to talk, but she got short answers. In the afternoon, Brian went back to Maisie's, and after a while he and Slanty fell asleep under the bush.

He got home late for supper. He slid into his seat and no one said anything. His mother served up a plate of beans, lukewarm now, pushed it toward him and lit another cigarette. Eve and Andy were still eating, but she had finished. Lately, she smoked more cigarettes at meals, and she didn't eat much. Pretty soon, she picked up her cup of coffee and the radio and moved into the living room.

Eve glared at Brian. "Why can't you get home on time?"

"Uh, I forgot."

"Forgot! You do it all the time—that's not forgetting."

"Today I fell asleep."

"Well, wake up! And ask someone what time it is. We always eat about five-thirty—there's some radio thing she listens to that ends at five."

"What's the matter. Is she . . ."

"Nothing, really." Eve's shoulders twitched restlessly. "She's not drinking, but she doesn't eat hardly anything. Just coffee. And there's something sort of crazy about the way she knits."

Andy said, "She's all right—she's taking the pills."

"Well . . ." They were talking quietly, leaning over the table, listening to the tinkling of the radio from the other room. Eve went on, "Anyway, get home on time. Anything might get her upset."

Brian tried. He asked Dwayne's mother, and Martha, too, to remind him when it was five o'clock. The library closed at five, so if he was there he could be home in plenty of time. Still some days he forgot, or if he went up to the radio station, he never quite figured how long it took to walk back.

One day he came home just as Eve and Andy were finishing dinner. His mother puffed out an angry cloud of smoke. "Git outa here! I'm sick of saving your food. You ain't here on time, you ain't eating!"

Without pause, Brian turned and slid back out to the street. He walked for a long time, keeping his mind blank. He didn't even go around to talk to Slanty. He just walked, until dark.

Then, he went home, tiptoed up the steps, and looked into the kitchen. Eve was there alone. He went in and she spoke angrily but softly, "See! I told you. You get her upset and she'll start again."

"Start what?"

"Drinking, stupid! You know that!"

"Well, it ain't my fault!" Brian's voice shot up and Eve shushed him. "I've been on time all week, until today! I was just a few minutes late . . ." He got out the bread and peanut butter.

She sighed. "I know. She doesn't make sense."

His voice went up again. "So what'm I supposed to do?"

"Hell!" Eve slapped the table and Brian jumped. Now *she* was getting upset, too. "How should I know? Just try, that's all!"

"O.K."

He went up and lay on his bed without even taking his clothes off. Andy was asleep; his mother's door was closed, but he could hear the low tinkling of the radio. What was she doing? Was it all starting over again? He remembered that movie about the surfers and the waves. Maybe that's the way it was. Smooth periods, and then the waves began, and got bigger, and bigger . . .

Brian jumped up. He couldn't lie on his bed all alone. He ran downstairs. "Listen, Eve . . . is she . . . is she really beginning again?"

"She hasn't yet. But this is the way she gets, when she really wants to drink. Only she can't, as long as she's taking those pills."

"Isn't there anything we can *do*?"

"Not really. Just take care of yourself. Get home on time."

Brian went back up to bed, took off his sneakers, and crawled in.

After that he tried to get home at five. Sometimes she put dinner on the table right away, sometimes not. Eve had stopped talking about her job, and even Andy's rambling accounts of movies he'd seen trailed off. The pill bottle that they'd almost stopped noticing became a magnet again. They couldn't help looking at it, until she took the pill. The silences got more tense, and one night she flipped the television on again and sat watching it, with her cigarette and coffee, while they ate silently.

In the daytime, Brian went his usual rounds, to Maisie's, to the park, to Martha's or Dwayne's. Everywhere there didn't seem to be anything to do. The afternoons got still and humid, until sometimes the sky suddenly darkened and thunder crashed. Dwayne and Brian would make a run for home, arriving just ahead of the storm if they were lucky. Panting inside the door one day, Dwayne said, "Man, I wish we had a real tornado!"

"Boy, don talk foolish!" his mother snapped.

"Well, I wish somethin happen! Brian, you know what? I be glad when school start! How bout you?"

"Yeah, I guess. When's it start?"

"Only bout two more weeks now."

Two more weeks, Brian thought, walking home that Friday. He felt sort of different about school now that there were kids he could talk to. Other people around, too, like at the radio station and the library and down at Soulard. He turned in at his corner, and unconsciously his steps slowed and his head went down. The one thing he didn't feel any different about was going home. At least he was on time—he knew he'd left Dwayne's at five.

He came in the kitchen door, and Eve was looking at a magazine with an empty plate in front of her, and Andy was finishing a bowl of Jell-O. Andy looked up sideways, half giggling, half scared.

Brian flashed a look at the TV. The local news was on. Angrily he said, "It's just after five. I'm not late!"

His mother banged her cup down and the coffee slopped over. "Don't tell me when I can get dinner! You be here!"

"How can I tell? I can't be here all the time!" Out of the corner of his eye, he could see Eve shaking her head at him, signaling. Looking at his mother, he knew something was wrong with her eyes, with her mouth, something wrong all over. Still he couldn't stop, he couldn't just take the blame.

"Why can't you stay home? Gotta be out on the street like a stray dog?" Before he could answer, she laughed suddenly, picked up his plate and put it on the floor. "Here, doggy!"

Andy giggled, unmistakably this time. Brian swung around. He'd been going to slip out the door, but now he welcomed the hot rush of anger, the cork pulled at last. He doubled up his clammy hands and started pounding Andy on the back.

"Cudditout! Leave 'im alone!" his mother hollered.

Brian spun around and kicked the plate of food. She was yelling at him, just the way she always used to yell. He stood right in front of her and yelled back: "Go ahead, get drunk, why don't you? Go ahead and kill yourself!"

Her hands smacked him, right and left. She was standing between him and the screen door, so he ran the other way, upstairs and into his room. He slammed the door and pulled the bureau over in front of it. He stood there, panting and sobbing, leaning on the bureau. Then he walked slowly to his bed and lay down on it, stiff, with his face pressed into the mattress.

Somehow, eventually, he came back to life, swung his legs around, and sat on the side of the bed. The streetlight shone in the window. The bureau stood in front of the door. Brian rubbed his hands over his face, shook his head, and stood up.

He started to push the bureau back. It made a loud rasping noise against the floor. He stopped and listened. No sound. He got the bureau back to its usual place and opened the door, listened again. He could hear the television.

He shivered, feeling suddenly cold, and turned back to find a sweatshirt. He stole down the stairs slowly, until he could look in the kitchen. Eve was sitting at the table and Andy was in front of the TV. There was no sound or light in the living room.

Brian moved into the kitchen, standing there stiff and silent, just inside the door. Eve looked up.

"Where is she?" Brian asked.

"Out," Eve said. "She's drinking again."

"It's not my fault! I wasn't late!" The whole scene came back to him. "I didn't do nothing—she hates me, that's all!"

Eve let out a long tired sigh. "I know—I didn't say it was your fault. Look—" She picked up their mother's pill bottle, opened it, and shook a few pills out in her hand.

Brian frowned. "What?"

"Look at them. Look close."

Brian picked one up and squinted at it. Letters were written in a circle around the edge, and he spelled them out, A S P I R I N. "Aspirin! Is that all they give her?"

"Unh-unh," Eve shook her head. "This isn't what they gave her—I saw her pills. They were capsules. But this is all she's taking now. I just noticed it last night."

Andy was staring at them. "Maybe she ran out of the good ones. Maybe we got to get more."

Eve said, "She got a new bottle last week. I saw it."

"She musta lost them!" Andy said. "I mean, that's the good stuff the doctor gave her. That's so she's gonna be O.K."

"What're those pills supposed to do?" Brian said. "Just make her feel better?"

"Unh-unh, I asked someone at work," Eve said. "They make it so you get sick, if you take even a sip of liquor. But she's stopped taking them, so now she can drink."

"You mean it won't hurt her?" Andy said.

Eve slapped the table, exasperated. "No—I mean now she'll get drunk again, just like before."

"But she doesn't want to!" Andy yelled. "She'd have to go in the hospital! She almost died before!"

"Yeah," Brian said softly.

Andy screamed at him. "You want her to! I heard what you said—'Go ahead and kill yourself!' You're the one who's driving her crazy! You're . . ."

The words were spinning around the room, and Brian plunged for the door. He wasn't just slipping away this time, he was running. A little way down the block, he heard Eve calling but he kept going, his sneakers slapping the sidewalk, his heart pounding. He had to keep going. There had to be someplace to go.

The only place he knew was old Maisie's yard, so he went there. There was no light in the window, and Slanty wasn't under the bush. His hole was there, the hollow he'd dug to keep cool in the daytime. Brian pressed his hip into the hollow and curled up in a ball.

chapter
sixteen

BRIAN WOKE UP stiff and cramped when
it began to get light. He couldn't think where he
was. Then he thought it must be afternoon, that
he'd dozed off under the bush with Slanty. But
Slanty wasn't there. Brian stretched and shivered
and remembered. He didn't want to remember,
so he curled up tight again and lay still until old
Maisie let the dog out. Slanty came and licked
his face, and pranced and wagged his tail, full of
early morning energy.

Brian stood up. He didn't know what to do,
but he didn't want anyone to see him and he
didn't want to think. With Slanty he moved

around to the back of old Maisie's house. He'd never been around there before—it was over-grown with weeds and bushes, and he could hardly see through into the other back yards. Good, he thought, no one will see me.

He went on around and discovered there was a little back porch, stacked with broken furniture and old flowerpots and garden tools. "Hey, Slanty, I could make a little house for us here!"

The dog barked and pranced. "Shhh-h!" Brian said. He went to work with sudden energy. He piled stuff that was no good into the bushes. There was a broom that would still sweep, and he got the porch all swept off. A long wicker sofa was missing one leg, but he propped it up with a flowerpot and turned a crate upside down to make a table. He found a cracked red vase and sat it in the middle of his table and put some flowers in it. He grinned. "Lookit, Slanty, ain't that pretty? We've got a nice place!"

The dog sat down and cocked his head on a slant, and his ears pricked up, just the way they had the first time Brian saw him. "That's my boy!" Brian crooned.

There was a faint noise from the front of the house, the door opening. "Here, girl, here, Queen-ie!" came the quavery voice. The dog scurried around the house instantly.

Brian's face fell. He looked at his "house" and knew it wasn't really a house. He perched on the edge of the wicker sofa tentatively, stretched out on it, wondering if he could sleep here. It wob-bled. He sat up, his hands hanging listlessly be-

tween his knees, and looked around. There was
no one in sight. The house opposite had a second-
story window that looked down on him, though,
and he wondered uneasily about that. Maybe
they'd call the police or something. He rocked
forward and became aware of his stomach,
empty. And all the time he was trying not to
think about the real problem, the big one.

He heard the front door open again, and he
whistled. His face lit up—Slanty had come back.
"Hey, boy, why don't you bring me something to
eat for a change?" Slanty wagged his tail indul-
gently, flopped on the porch in the early-morning
sun, and went to sleep. Brian said, "Mmm, it's all
right for you—she gave you breakfast."

He stood up and stretched and dug his hands
in his pockets. His eyes lit up. There was some
change in his pocket, left from getting milk at
the store the day before. He thought, Suppose
someone sees me? Then he shook his head and
answered himself, That's crazy—I'm not hiding.
I didn't do anything wrong.

He went to the store, the store he and Martha
had gone to, run by the Greek man. It was the
opposite direction from home. The man had just
opened up, and there was no one else in the
store. Brian got a soda, a bag of potato chips, a
cup cake, and a candy bar. He looked at them
and at his money and went back for a second
soda. He'd get thirsty later, when it was hot.

He walked back toward old Maisie's, not hurrying any, because the long day stretched ahead
of him with nothing to do but fool around on

that back porch. He fished a torn movie magazine out of a trash can.

He read the magazine, found a little more
furniture for his porch, and retreated under the
shady bush with Slanty when the sun got hot.
They slept most of the afternoon.

Slanty roused up suddenly and ran away.
Brian sat up, yawned, and saw old Maisie on the
porch. He came half out from the shade of the
bush, and Slanty darted back and forth, between
him and Maisie.

"Who's that? Who's that there? Get away from
here!" Old Maisie gripped her cane and tried to
make her voice threatening.

"It's me, ma'am. Brian. Uh, Bobby. You know,
I come to see the dog."

"Here, Queenie. Come here, dearie," she called
fretfully.

"I call him Slanty—he holds his head that
way." Brian whistled, but the dog stayed with
old Maisie.

"She's my Queenie. Come, dearie, shall we get
our supper?" Old Maisie moved toward the door,
and the dog followed her, tail wagging.

Suddenly Brian couldn't bear it, and he hurried to the porch and started talking: "Ma'am, I
wanted to ask you something. See, my family
went away for a day or two. I wonder, can I
sleep on the back porch—Slanty could sleep
there with me—I got it all fixed up. I won't be no
trouble, ma'am."

"Back porch?" She picked those two words out

and shook her head worriedly. "Back porch? That's where Clerow keeps his garden tools. He won't let anyone touch them."

"I didn't hurt anything, ma'am. Uh, where does . . . uh, Queenie sleep?"

"She sleeps on my bed, don't you, dearie? Come along. Boy, you better go home; it's getting late."

"Ma'am!" Brian's voice went up. "Could I come inside a minute?"

"They've all gone away, boy. Jamie's gone to Tulsa, Esther lives in California, there's no one here anymore."

"That's all right. Maybe I could help you with something, like cleaning up, or moving stuff."

"They don't come here anymore. You better go home, boy; your mother will be hunting for you."

"Ma'am, that's what I mean! See, she's gone away. Can I stay for a little while?"

"Your mother . . . let's see that must be Lydia Holloway. Likely she's gone to see her sister, Olive. Olive was always sickly. . . ." Old Maisie opened her door and moved inside, talking to people of the past and forgetting Brian. But she let him follow her into the house.

Off the entrance hall, an arch opened into a big room. There was no light on in there, but Brian could make out a piano and other big pieces of furniture, all covered with dust sheets, and rows of straight chairs, empty. His shoulders wriggled, and he looked away. To the other side of the hall, a door opened. A light was on in there.

Slanty ran ahead, then turned, crouched, and barked expectantly.

"We're coming, dearie. We don't often have company, do we? Queenie, this is Lydia Holloway's boy." The old lady hobbled slowly into the room and Brian followed.

The lampshade on the one lamp was pink, and the room had a rosy look. Two chairs were up front by the window—that was where she sat to look out from behind the curtain. Brian peered around. A clothesline ran straight across the room, and it was draped with old-lady underwear. Embarrassed, Brian dropped his eyes. There in a corner by the bed was a chamber pot. He'd never seen a real one before, only the ones in jokes.

He cleared his throat and stood uncertainly. Old Maisie moved toward the back of the room, ducking under the clothesline with surprising adroitness. Brian heard water running, and a match lit, and all the time she was talking along to herself. Slanty sat looking at her, occasionally flicking his head around to check on Brian, too. Cautiously, Brian eased himself into the chair by the window, and Slanty jumped up in the other chair and curled up in the hollow that was just his shape. Brian plucked the curtain and peeped out. He grinned. No one could see him, but he could see everything on the street.

Old Maisie shuffled back to the front of the room and put down a bowl for the dog. Slanty jumped out of the chair, and Brian got up quickly, too.

"My goodness, you startled me, boy! What are you doing here?"

"Uh—I just came in for a bit, remember?"

"Hmm, humm," she clucked. "We're having our cereal. Do you want a bowl of cereal, boy?"

"Yes, thank you, ma'am."

"Come along then."

Brian followed her to the back of the room, where there was a sink and a hot plate. The room had a funny musty smell. She spooned cereal into a bowl, and it was white and steaming, not like any cereal he'd seen before. He blew on it and carried it back to the front and sat down in the dog's chair.

Old Maisie laughed suddenly, a thin cackle. "He's sitting in your chair, Queenie, he's eating your porridge! Heh, heh, heh!" She ate her own cereal, occasionally talking to herself or the dog, not to Brian. When she was finished, she plucked the corner of the curtain and looked out and went on talking.

Brian chirped to Slanty, and the dog jumped in his lap. They all sat there for quite a long time. Old Maisie let the curtain drop and dozed in her chair. Slanty slept. Brian sat stiff and quiet.

The old lady's eyes opened and she looked at Brian and the dog and continued talking, as if there had been no interruption. "We go to bed early, don't we, dearie? You can let the dog out for a minute, boy."

Brian went out and around to the back. It was still light out and someone might see him. Soon the dog heard Maisie calling and ran back to the front door. Brian followed, and stepped inside the house.

"Tch, tch, what are we going to do, boy? Hannah hasn't cleaned the spare room this week." She puttered down the hall and turned on a tiny light in the shape of a candle. It only made the shadows in the big room worse. "You'll have to sleep on the couch."

She flipped the sheet off one of the ghostly shapes and a cloud of dust went up. "Tch, tch, that girl never cleans properly, I'll have to get after her!" She leaned over and ran her hand over the fabric of the couch. Brian saw that it was covered with a velvety material, with gold threads running through it.

"My mother ordered the material from Paris." Old Maisie stood up and said the words quietly, and she looked across the room as if she could see it filled with elegantly dressed ladies and gentlemen.

Abruptly, she said, "Come along, dearie, it's late. Don't forget to use the bathroom, boy; it's just down the hall. Take your shoes off. Come along, Queenie."

She moved surprisingly fast sometimes, and in a moment she had gone in the other room and shut the door. Brian was alone in the ghostly parlor. Gingerly, he sat on the edge of the sofa. It squeaked, and he sprang up. Suddenly he knew he couldn't sleep here. He tiptoed to the door. It wasn't locked on the inside, and he slipped out and stood on the steps. He'd been holding his breath. He sighed with relief now. He was out.

He squatted down on the front step. A few passersby walked along the street in the gray evening light, but they didn't look at him. He leaned over, hugging his ribs, as if to warm the cold ball in the middle of his stomach.

All the pictures he'd been trying to forget came back: the dish of food he'd kicked across the kitchen, his mother yelling, the pill with A S P I R I N on it, Andy yelling . . . Andy couldn't help it, he was just a kid. Eve and Andy, they were his family, he ought to go home. But he couldn't make up his mind, couldn't make his feet walk there.

He rocked back and forth on the step, hugging only himself.

chapter
seventeen

MELVITA CLOSED her bedroom door, put
a chair in front of it, and got her money out of
her secret place. She wasn't exactly distrustful,
she just knew if a person needed money bad
enough, they'd have to borrow it. Sometimes
she'd leave money in her pocketbook, and later
her mother would say, "Vita, honey, I borrow ten
dollars from you. I pay you back, O.K.?" And
Melvita would say, "O.K." After all, what else
could you say? Her mother needed the money,
and she'd pay it back if there was any way to,
but mostly there wasn't.

Now she counted out eighty-seven dollars and fifty cents. She looked at it proudly for a minute, then sighed. It was never enough. Once you got in a store, you always needed more. The thing you really wanted most was too expensive. And you couldn't just buy things for yourself and come home and see Melissa and Pet standing there puckering their mouths.

She'd have to take Melissa shopping this year, too—she was getting big enough to choose her own clothes. Melvita folded the bills carefully and put them back in their place. She thought of taking out one dollar for spending, but decided against it. That was one good thing about going out with Anthony; he had money to spend. Not like old Dwayne.

Melvita sat on the bed she'd just made, then sprawled back on it and stretched luxuriously and considered going back to sleep. She thought about Anthony. He was cute. Going with a high-school dude was sure different than playing around with boys like Dwayne. She yawned. Staying out late all the time made you tired, though.

She almost dozed, then jumped up and shook herself. She didn't have to mind Precious today, and she wasn't going to waste her free day sleeping. She went in the bathroom, looked at herself, and started brushing her hair down hard. She wet the brush. As soon as she brushed one side down, the other side jumped up. She gave up and went downstairs.

EMILY CHENEY NEVILLE

"You come home some decent hour, maybe you could get up in the morning, help with the work!" Her mother started in right away.

"I does my share round here," Melvita said. She opened the refrigerator and started to take out a soda.

"You leave that Coke—it the last one!"

"I go get more."

"You leave it, hear? Get yoself some cereal, then you clean up that bathroom!"

"I don't want no cereal, and I ain't the one leave that bathroom a mess! How come Melissa don ever clean it up?"

"She be watching Rodney, and don't stick your lip out at me, girl!"

Melvita slammed the refrigerator door shut and ran back up the stairs. She charged into the bathroom, dragged the laundry and the stool and scales out, and started banging the broom into the corners. She scoured the tub and basin and toilet and put the furniture back in place with loud thumps. She went back into her own room and cleaned that up, too. By the time she was finished, she felt quite cheerful, and hungry.

Her mother had gone out. Melvita found a few bits of ham left in the icebox and started frying them up. The good smell filled the kitchen, and pretty soon Melissa and Pet and Rodney came in.

"Sure smell good when you cook," Pet said.

"Some! Some!" Rodney's mouth opened like a baby bird's.

Melissa said righteously, "Momma could be wanting that ham for dinner."

"Can't do nothing by myself, can I!" Melvita said, but the others knew it was only pretend grumbling, because she got out four plates and plunked them on the counter. She stirred eggs into the pan and made toast. They all sat down.

Their mother came in and put two big bags of groceries down. "Hmm, smell good! Least I won't have to fix no lunch. Time I get through lugging groceries, I don't even want to look at food!"

"You want some of this, Momma? There be plenty," Melvita said, and it was a sort of apology.

"Thank you, honey—I just going to have that Coke. I been counting on it. You can go get some more, after—I couldn't carry nothing more."

"I'll go, Momma, can I?" Melissa said.

"Nope, you going to help me do the laundry."

"Aw . . ." Melissa pouted and pushed her plate with the last few bites on it away from her. Pet reached to take a bit of ham, and Melissa slapped her hand. Melvita smiled tolerantly and cleared the table.

"C'mon, Rodney, you want to go to the store with me?" she said.

"Go! Go!"

Melvita picked him up and started out the door but Rodney started kicking and screeching: "Self! Self!" She put him down, and when he reached the front step he turned around and backed laboriously down it, puffing and grunting.

"You the cutest little black cat in the whole world!" Melvita scooped him up and kissed him.

After they got the sodas, she looked over in the park and saw Martha there. She settled herself on the bench and said, "Here we be! You want a soda—they cold, we just get 'em."

"Unh-unh." Martha shook her head.

"What the matter, girl—you in the dumps this morning?"

"Maybe."

"I know—you be thinkin about dietin again. That always gets you gloomy. Is you getting fatter again?"

"I ain't!" Martha flared up. "I ain't fatter!" She hesitated. "Am I?"

"Unh-unh." Melvita shrugged. "Look the same to me."

"Melvita, listen—" But Melvita interrupted.

"What we going to do tonight? Go to Happy's first?"

"I guess."

Melvita yawned. "I be getting tired, staying out so late all the time. You know . . . all that."

"Yeah, I know. Melvita . . ."

"What we goin do when school start? You think Anthony and James come round same as always? Maybe they be goin with the chicks in high school?"

"How do I know what goin to happen?" Martha snapped.

Melvita shook her head. "Girl, you really got the hump today! Well, I got to go home—Rodney look like he falling asleep. Seeya tonight."

"Seeya."

When she went in the kitchen, Melissa looked up with a smug smile. "Momma leave you a note," she said and poked the folded bit of paper toward Melvita. Melvita knew she'd read it.

"Huh!" Melvita picked it up and read the few words. She stamped her foot. "Of all the mean tricks! How she know I can stay home with you brats this evening? Maybe I got a date!"

Righteously, Melissa said, "You went last night. Momma got to have her turn—she like to have some fun, too."

"You just wait! Another year, and you be the one left holding the bag! I be outa here!"

"You goin 'way, Melvita?" Pet looked up at her with big eyes. "Where you goin?"

"I don't know where I'm goin, but I'm on my way!" She looked down and patted Pet on the head. "Not today, baby. Someday." She shot a glare at Melissa. "You there, you peel the potatoes for supper! I got things to do upstairs. Rodney, he sleepin on the couch."

She went up to her room and shut the door. In a way, it was nice to have a whole evening to herself, with no hurrying to get ready and get out. She wondered if Anthony would be sore when she didn't show up. Maybe he get himself another chick, she thought. She turned the idea over in her head and then she stood up straight and stared in the mirror and smiled. I don't mind if he do. He be some fun, but I don't really care what he do.

They ate supper, and after the others were all settled watching TV, Melvita went out on the front step. It was getting dark. It was sort of nice and quiet. Nights like this, Melvita thought, when I be stuck home, Dwayne used to come round. He bring his little radio, and we be sittin here listenin, just us two.

She hunched her shoulders up and didn't feel so peaceful anymore.

chapter
eighteen

AFTER MELVITA LEFT the park, Martha
sat on the bench alone, thinking about her own
problem. She'd wanted to talk to Melvita. Or had
she? Anyway, the words hadn't come out.

"Why you looking sad, Martha?" Katie hung
on her knee. "C'mon, us go home."

"O.K., honey." They walked home, and Martha went into the living room. The television was
on, turned low, and it was quiet in there, just
Martha and her father. He was reading his newspaper, and Martha sat down and picked at her
nails with a nail file.

Her father had his shoes off, because he stood

up all day working in the drugstore, and when he got through his feet hurt. He was a tidy man. He even sat in his chair neatly, not sprawled, his necktie neatly folded on the arm of the chair and those elastic things still around his sleeves.

Martha looked at him and suddenly saw him. She thought, I live with this man every day of my life, but I don't know what he be like. He so quiet. He don't be drinking up the beer and cussin and hollerin, like some kids' daddy. He don't really say much. What he be thinkin inside there, all the time?

What he think about me? Supposin I open my mouth right now and say, "Daddy, I be goin to have a baby."

She looked at him, and she knew she couldn't say it. She couldn't say that to him. She could tell her mother first, and her mother would cry and scold, and then she'd tell her father, and Martha would never know what he thought. And after a while, they'd all just get used to the idea that there was going to be another baby in the family.

Martha shook her head vigorously. That isn't the way I want it to happen, she thought. It's all wrong that way. If I be goin to have a baby, it's James's baby and mine, and we be proud of it, and we come tell Daddy and Momma together, and then it be our baby.

She stamped her foot firmly on the floor, and her father looked up mildly over the top of his glasses. She smiled at him, and he went back to his newspaper.

So I got to talk to James, Martha thought, that

be the first thing to do. When I see him tonight, I tell him. But right away she knew it wasn't going to be so easy. Somehow, James was so busy about a whole lot of other things. He wasn't ready to think about a baby. She sighed and felt alone.

The TV announcer went to a loud, jingly commercial about a shampoo, and Martha sat up straight in her chair and shook her head. Martha, you be plain foolish! You prob'ly ain't pregnant at all. Just two weeks late, that ain't nothin. Time nough to talk to James when you be sure.

She got up and snapped the television off and her father looked up questioningly. She said, "Anyone in your drugstore ask for that Goldy Shampoo, you sell 'em somethin else! That commercial is an ir-ritation!"

When Martha got to Happy's that night it was later than usual, but Melvita wasn't there. James was busy talking, and in a few minutes Anthony came up to her. "Where that Melvita?" he asked, as if she ought to know.

"Man, that girl ain't got no keeper! I don't know where she at!"

Anthony frowned in mock anger. "I don't like no chicks keep me waitin!"

"You can lump it then!" She didn't really mean to speak crossly, but she didn't feel like kidding with Anthony either.

"Girl, I reckon you feelin evil tonight," he said and moved away.

Martha leaned back against the fence and fanned herself. She looked over toward James, caught his eye for a minute, and then looked idly over the rest of the group. Look who turn up, she said to herself, ole Dwayne. He finally come back. Wonder what he got to say for hisself.

She watched him standing by himself, just listening to James like the others. He caught her eye, then looked away. Well, I ain't shy, Martha said and walked over to him.

"Hey, Dwayne, what happenin?"

"Oh, same ole." He nodded his head toward James. "You know this cat?"

"Yeah, sure." Funny, she thought, Dwayne the only cat don't know bout me and James.

"He pretty hip," Dwayne said.

"Sure. Where you been at, all summer, Dwayne?"

"Working. Here and there. I be readin some books, too."

"Yeah?" She laughed. "How come you do that?"

"Jus happen, it do." He didn't meet her eye, but he was looking past her, his eyes running over the bunch of kids. He'd been free to go out in the evening for a while now, but this was the first time he'd got his nerve up to go to Happy's. He wanted to see Melvita, but then, too, he didn't want to see her with some other dude. He kept looking now, relieved and disappointed at once, because she wasn't there.

"Seeya round," Martha said and moved away, because she saw that the bunch around James had broken up. She and James leaned against the fence, and Martha fanned the still air. She couldn't start talking to James, not really—there were too many kids talking and laughing nearby.

"You want to come over to Northside?" James said. "Some cats I got to talk to."

"I don't want to go nowhere. I hope they be a big crashing thunderstorm, and it cool off, and I get a good long sleep."

"You don't got to wish no thunderstorm on me —I got to walk!" he laughed, and she thought, He don't even notice I ain't feeling good.

"I see you tomorrow, O.K., girl?" She said O.K. and he kissed her and went off down the hill. Martha looked after him and thought, One more person I manage not to talk to. She walked away from Happy's, restless and not wanting to go home. Walking out under the streetlights, she set off around the park.

As she went past old Maisie's, she glanced up to see if the old lady was watching from the window. The window was dark, but then the streetlight caught the glint of Brian's pale hair.

Martha hurried up to the fence. She whispered hoarsely, "Brian! Boy—what you doin there?"

Brian looked up, stared. "Ohh. Hi."

"What you doin, sittin there in the dark? You best get on home!"

Brian got up and walked down to the gate. "You can come in. She's gone to sleep; she won't holler at you."

"Where yo little dog? You just hangin round by yo own self?"

"Mmm. Yeah. Hey, come around back—I'll show you my place I fixed up."

EMILY CHENEY NEVILLE

They walked around, and Brian sat on the
wicker couch and stretched his legs out. "See, I
can sleep here."

Martha stared at the couch, and then at the
vase with the flower in it. She shook her head
slowly. "Brian, what you tryin to do? Quit foolin
me."

"I thought I could . . . well, like live here."

Martha sat down, planted her feet firmly, and
leaned forward, looking right at Brian. "Cut out
that mumble talk! You run away from home, that
it?"

"I guess."

"You don't guess—you know! When you
leave?"

"Last night, uh, maybe two nights."

"You sleep here two nights already?"

"I slept under the bush, you know, where
Slanty sleeps."

"What you do that for? Your momma get
drunk again?"

"I guess."

"Guess!" Martha stamped her foot loudly, and
Brian said, "Sh-h." Martha went on: "All right, I
be quiet. Now what happen—either yo momma
be drinkin, or she ain't?"

"She got mad at me. She told me to eat my
dinner on the floor like a dog. I got mad, and she
hit me. Then I locked myself in my room. When
I came out, finally, Eve said she went out, and
she's going to get drunk, because she don't take
those pills anymore."

Martha tried to digest all that. It didn't make much sense, but she knew that asking questions, getting details, wasn't going to help. Finally she said, "I guess you was pretty scared, huh?"

"Yeah." He sat for a minute and went on. "I was scared when I left, and now I'm scared to go back. What am I going to do?"

"Well, playin house, like—that ain't goin to help."

"Slanty isn't even out here at night. There's no one."

"Pffoo! That just a dog! You can't fix your life round no dog!"

"So what am I going to do?"

Martha stood up. "Come on, I'll walk long toward yo house with you."

"What if . . ."

Martha stepped off the porch, just as the sky lit up with a flash of lightning. The crack of thunder followed so instantly that it blasted her back on the porch. She grabbed Brian by the shoulders. "Lordy, that scare me!"

"That was close! Maybe some tree in the park got hit."

"Lordy," Martha moaned. "Why I have to wish a thunderstorm on us? Brian, what if we have a tornado?"

"Aw, we ain't having a tornado—that's just on those signs in school. Lookit, here comes the rain."

It came, as suddenly as the lightning had, first a few huge splatting drops, than a sheet of water falling between them and the house next door.

"Oh, poor James. I hope he get inside," Martha said.

"Huh?"

"James. That my boy friend I was tellin you bout." She paused, then pulled Brian down to sit beside her on the rickety couch. "Brian, I got to tell you somethin. I got to tell somebody. Maybe I be goin to have a baby."

"Baby? You?"

"You hear. Me."

"I mean—how come . . ."

Martha stamped her foot. "I ain't gotta splain to you how babies come, do I?"

"No, I mean . . . well, I didn't know you were old enough."

"Course I's ole nough!"

"Oh." Brian stared out at the sheets of rain and tried to figure it out. Of course he'd seen pregnant women on the street, and he glanced at Martha now. "How do you know? You don't look . . . well, like that."

Martha laughed but the rain drowned the sound. "You crazy, boy. I know when I don't get my period."

Brian shifted ground. "You know how to take care of a baby?"

"Sure, anybody know that."

"You gonna get married?"

The question hung there, and after a while Martha said, "I ain't even sure yet. I didn't tell James yet."

Brian said dreamily, "It'd be nice to have a baby."

Martha looked at him and she thought, Brian's the only boy in the world would say that. She went along in his dream world. "If it be a boy, I think I name him Lionel. A girl—maybe Stephanie. Maybe Vanessa, that be pretty."

"Where you going to live?" Brian said.

Martha stood up, suddenly impatient. "No sense in this kinda talk! I don't know what I goin do bout nothin! Time enough to think when I be *sure*. What I be sure bout is you and me got to get home!"

"It's raining," Brian said, hunching back.

"It goin to stop. See, it just ordinary rain now."

"I'm scared."

Martha looked at him, and she knew he didn't mean the thunderstorm. She said, "I know. Me, too. But ain't no use stayin' here playin house and makin up names—we gotta go home and do whatever we gotta do. Yo sister be worryin. Maybe your momma ain't drunk, and she be worryin, too. Pretty soon *my* momma be worryin. C'mon."

"O.K." Brian was relieved to get started toward home, as long as she got him moving. They walked through the dripping grass and out onto the street. A soft rain was still falling, and steam rose from the hot pavement. The air was cooler.

"Night," Martha said at the corner. "You come round and tell me what happen tomorrow, hear?"

"Yeah, you, too. Night." He walked along his own street, feeling as if he'd been away a long, long time.

He inched up the stairs to the kitchen slowly,

listening, wondering who was there and what they were going to say to him. He paused at the last step, finally got his courage up, and stepped to the door.

No one was there. There was just the television, chattering. Brian stood inside the kitchen and looked around. The dishes were washed. The place looked tidy. He moved silently across the room to the hall, listening and looking, but not calling. He came to the door of the living room.

It was empty. Her chair was there under the light with the knitting hung over the arm. Brian walked toward it and picked the knitting up, for no real reason—he wasn't interested in what she knitted.

He held it up. The knitting hung from his hands and coiled on the floor, long and ugly. It must have been six feet long, with wool of many colors—garish greens, neon pink, and mustard yellow—no shape or pattern or sense to it. Maybe she had intended it to be a scarf, but no one could put that thing around his neck. Brian dropped it.

He turned back to the kitchen. As he entered from the hall, the screen door squeaked and there was Eve. She stood and stared at him.

Andy pushed from behind her. He yelled, "Gosh! She's had me walking all over, hunting for you! Where were you?"

"Brian Moody!" Eve found her voice and it was hot and angry. "You do that one more time, and I'm calling the police right off! They can keep you!"

"Police?" Brian picked up the word. "I didn't do nothing."

"Just disappeared, that's all! Where you been?"

"I went over where that dog is—you know, the one she wouldn't let me keep."

"I didn't know you found him," Andy said. "Who's is he?"

"Old Maisie's."

"You stayed with her?" Andy looked goggle-eyed, then snickered.

"Oh, shut up, Andy!" Eve snapped. "I don't care who she is—we've got trouble enough here, without you cutting out!"

"Where's Mom?" Brian asked.

"Out. She wasn't too bad last night—just sort of woozy." Eve sighed. "I guess she'll be worse tonight."

Andy said, "Maybe she just went to the store. Maybe she's visiting someone—you don't know!"

"Yeah, maybe," Eve said listlessly. Then she swung around and faced Andy. "Look, Andy, I know you're just a kid . . ."

"I'm eleven!"

". . . yeah, well anyway, you quit fooling yourself. Mom's a drunk. Maybe sometime she'll stop herself, maybe she'll have to go to the hospital again, but that's the way she is. Don't pretend she's out buying your sugar frosty flakes!"

Andy's mouth quivered and he didn't say anything.

Eve said to Brian, "I really was just going to call the police—then Andy remembered where your girl friend lived."

"Huh?"

"Martha. She said she'd been with you."

"I wasn't with her all the time . . ."

"I didn't say you were! You haven't got that much sense! She said you were with some old dog."

"I couldn't help it. I had to go somewhere."

"Yeah, I know. But we've got to hold together. Listen, Brian, you promise me—"

"Yeah, I won't go away again," Brian said.

"What if . . ." Andy was still standing there looking shaky. "What if Mom doesn't get home?"

"She will," Eve said. "She always has."

Brian said, "There's no use waiting—we'll worry about it in the morning. Come on, Andy, let's go to bed."

As long as someone told him what to do, Andy felt better. He followed Brian up the stairs. They lay in their beds, and Brian told Andy about old Maisie's ghostly room and the little place he'd fixed on the back porch. "I'll show you tomorrow," he said. "She's used to me. She thinks I belong to some old friend of hers. She gave me dinner even. Some funny-looking warm cereal stuff."

"Is she really crazy?" Andy asked.

"She's all right. She just forgets things—like what year it is, or who you are."

"I bet you were scared in that room, huh?"

"Yeah."

"Yeah, me, too. I would be."

They fell asleep.

Brian came downstairs in the morning, and there she was, sitting at the kitchen table with a cup of coffee. She looked at him dully and took another tiny sip of coffee. He realized she didn't know he'd been away. It was just another morning. She got up suddenly and hurried upstairs to the bathroom.

Eve came down. "She's being sick."

"She was down here. She had coffee."

Eve looked at the cup and nodded. In a little while, they heard the slow steps on the stairs, and she came into the kitchen. She reached for the bottle of pills in the middle of the table and shook one out into her hand. It was a little striped capsule. She swallowed it down, looked at her two children almost scornfully, and went into the other room. They heard the radio turn on and the sigh of the chair as she sat down.

Eve and Brian moved out onto the porch, where Andy was sitting with his bowl of cereal. Eve said, "She took one of her pills again, the real ones."

Andy looked up and grinned. "Then she's gonna be all right? She ain't gonna drink anymore, right?"

Eve looked at him, and her face was hard. "Wrong. Look, Andy, quit trying to hang that on me! I'm not going to keep cheering you up and saying everything's peachy!"

"But—"

"But she's an alcoholic, that's what. Sometimes she'll be better, sometimes she'll be worse."

"She ain't going to be really better, ever?" Andy's voice cracked and he put his spoon down and covered his face with his hands.

Eve wouldn't give in. She said, "Don't ask me —I don't know! I just try to live with her, any way I can."

Andy sobbed. Eve looked at him a moment but she wouldn't give in. She went back in the house. Brian sat down on the step beside Andy. After a while Andy was just sniffling, and Brian reached out and touched him lightly. "You wanna go over and see that place, I was telling you?"

Andy wiped his face on his T-shirt sleeve and stood up. "O.K.," he said.

chapter
nineteen

MARTHA STRETCHED and opened her eyes, and she couldn't believe it was morning. She had slept the whole night away in one gulp, not tossing and dreaming and waking up the way she had been doing. She lay back, feeling good all over.

She got up finally and went in the bathroom. She yawned, smiled at herself in the mirror, and sat down on the toilet. Then she saw.

All the worries of the past two weeks whirled through her head, like a movie playing backward, then forward again to here, now, free, safe.

She put her face in her hands and said, "Oh, praise God! Thank you!"

No one would have to be told about the baby —there wouldn't be any baby. No need to talk to James, no need for her mother to feel bad, no need to wonder what her father was thinking. Then she stopped and thought, I wish I'd told James, I wish we could . . . She pushed the idea out of her head.

She got dressed and hurried down to the kitchen. "Mornin, Momma! Sure is a pretty day!"

"I guess you're right—I didn't notice. That why you looking so happy?"

"I guess. Seem like everythin gettin ready to start again—summer be almost gone. I got to buy me some new school clothes. Goin get me a size fourteen!"

"That be good, honey. What you want me to fix you for breakfast?"

"Melon and maybe one boiled egg, just a little one."

She called up Melvita and they decided to meet in the park. Martha brought the newspaper to look at the advertisements for school clothes.

"What happen you ain't at Happy's last night?" she asked.

"My momma went out and I have to stay home. What you do?"

"Nothin much. I talk to James awhile, but he goin to a meeting, and I start home, and I see that Brian at ole Maisie's, and we be talking while the thunderstorm was carryin on. Before that, Anthony, he ask where you was at. I told him I ain't yo keeper."

Melvita giggled.

Cautiously, Martha said, "You know who be at Happy's last night?"

Melvita's heart gave a little bounce. "Who?"

"Dwayne, that who."

Melvita kept her voice disinterested. "Who he with?"

"Ain't with no one. Jus hangin round."

"He stay long?"

"I don't know. I guess I left first. You goin tonight?"

Melvita thought a minute. "Yeah, I be there."

Melvita walked home slowly, thinking. She went upstairs and into the bathroom and locked the door. It was the only really private place. She looked at herself in the mirror and poked at her hair. She frowned. It didn't fluff out like an Afro, it just poked out. She grabbed a handful of it and combed it together and reached into the drawer for one of her old pieces of yarn. She tied that to her topknot and nodded at herself. She liked the familiar feeling of it pulling against her scalp.

After supper, she didn't hurry. She didn't want to get to Happy's too early. Finally she set off, and as she came near she saw Martha and James and the high-school kids down at the corner. She looked past them, toward the kids right in front of Happy's, and she saw Dwayne. He kept turning his head, looking up and down the street. Melvita looked away before their eyes met. She felt the pulse thumping in her neck, and she wasn't sure what to do first.

She didn't have to decide really. Anthony stepped out of the bunch at the corner, reached out and flipped the topknot on her head.

"Girl, what you got there? You some kinda pumpkin, with a handle on top?" He took hold of it.

Melvita yanked her head away. "Keep yo big ole hand outa my hair!"

"You im-plying my hand ain't clean nough?"

"I ain't im-plying, or sup-plying, nothin!"

Anthony stood back a little, with his hands in his pockets, and when he spoke his voice was silky. "How come I don't see you here last night? You tell me you goin to be here. I don't like it when my chick tell me one thing, do somethin else."

"You don't see me cause I ain't here. I was busy."

"You goin to be busy, girl, I could be busy my own self."

They looked at each other, glassy-eyed, for just a second. Neither one cared enough to have a real fight. Melvita tossed her head and walked slowly up toward Happy's.

Anthony turned back to the high-school kids, and the crowd closed around him. Nobody had to say it; they just all knew Melvita and Anthony had split.

Martha and James were standing a little apart,

and Martha watched Melvita walk away. "Mmm-hmm, summer be almost over, yessirree!"

"What you mumblin about, girl?"

"I just be thinkin that maybe Melvita goin back to her ole boy friend."

"She split with Anthony?"

"Seems like."

"Don't you get ideas like that. You be stayin. Right here with me."

"Yeah." They leaned together, holding hands. Martha said, "Let's not go to any meetin or anythin tonight. We could just go over in the park, where we can sit and talk."

"O.K.," he said.

"Hey, Melvita!" Sharon sang out, and the little knot of girls opened and closed around Melvita. They talked about her new shoes and Corita's new hairdo, and what was going to happen at school.

Gloria said, "Who we going to get for the new eighth-grade teacher, anyone know?"

"Martha saw him—she say he look cool. She was over there registering Katie."

"He black?"

"Uh-huh. And hip. He got an Afro and a baad shirt!"

"He real young?" Gloria's eyes lit up.

"Unh-unh— He the dis-tinguished type; he ain't no kid!" Melvita's eyes roved over the heads of the other girls, and there was Dwayne, watching her. Their eyes caught, held for a moment. Melvita said casually to the girls, "I got to see ole

Dwayne—ain't see him all summer. Don't go, you all."

She walked toward him, feeling the cool night air tickling her scalp. "Hey!" she said to him.

"Hey, girl! What happenin?"

"Same ole, same ole. Place sorta quiet here."

Dwayne grinned and did a fast tap-skip with his feet. "Guess it get pretty dead, when I ain't round."

"Is that what you guess? So where you been at?" She said it lightly, but he knew she was asking a real question.

"I get messed up with my ole man. Stay out late one night and bam! He catch me up side of my head and I can't go out for a month! He just like to put me on a punishment!"

Melvita remembered that night, early in the summer, and she wasn't going to be put off that easily. "What you doin out so late? You was goin to meet me here, member that?"

"Yeah." Dwayne looked down, making circles on the sidewalk with his toe. "I get in some trouble with some cats down to the project. Maybe I tell you bout it sometime."

"Bad trouble?"

"Mmmm—"

"Police?"

He shook his head.

She said, "You couldn't call me up even?"

"I shoulda, I know. I just . . . I jus couldn . . ." He looked at her, begging her to understand.

Melvita nodded. "That James—he the big one,

down there with Martha—he say police be beating on dudes all the time, no reason."

"Yeah, I listen to him last night. He be a cool cat."

"Police get you, you gotta know what to do. You gotta find out them things."

"That be what I goin to do this year, goin find out a lot of things. I be in the library some this summer, they got some cool books."

"We got a real cool new teacher at school—he know a lot of things."

"He black?"

"Sure."

The radio in the candy store tuned up with a hot beat, and several of the kids started moving. Dwayne took Melvita. "C'mon, girl, I ain't dance all summer!"

Next morning, Martha remembered Brian hadn't come around. Just like that boy, she thought, he don't tell me nothin, probably sittin and moonin on Maisie's porch again. His sister now, she act real nice and sensible. Maybe I go round to his house, my own self.

She thought about it, but she felt uneasy about Brian's mother, and she didn't want to go alone. She called up Melvita.

Melvita said, "I tell Dwayne I meet him this mornin."

"Where he go, huh? You find out?"

"He didn't go nowhere. He get in some trouble. Bad trouble I guess. He wouldn't tell me what."

"I knew something musta happen. Didn't make sense, he jus disappear."

"Well, he O.K. now. He get kinda serious. He tell me bout books he be readin."

"Yeah, he tell me that, too. Why don't you come over here, and we go round to his house?"

They went to Dwayne's, and Mrs. Yale gave them cookies and sodas. When they finished Martha said, "How bout we walk round to Rutger Street? I want to see how that Brian be doin."

Dwayne said, "He be doin like always. I see him in the library."

"Yeah? You know Brian? He readin books, too?"

"Nah, he don't read no books. He play checkers."

"You know bout his momma?"

"I don't know nothin bout his momma," Dwayne said.

"She be sick. You know, she got the bottle sickness. She go in the hospital once already. Maybe she goin again."

"O.K., come on, we go see," Dwayne said.

"I didn't want go alone," Martha said. "His momma, she also don't like colored."

"Black," Dwayne said.

"Well, anyway, she don't like us."

"She goin holler at us?" Melvita said.

"Aw, you jus go ring the doorbell," Dwayne said. "Say, 'Scuse me, ma'am, I be takin orders for the Girl Scout cookies.' She can't holler at the Girl Scouts."

Melvita giggled. When they got to Brian's house, Dwayne and Melvita stood on the sidewalk, and Martha climbed the stairs. Eve was alone in the kitchen. She looked up and smiled. "Oh, hello! Come on in."

"I just come to ask about Brian." Martha stood uncertainly just inside the kitchen door. "He come home all right, did he?"

"Yeah, he's here. Hey, Brian!" She turned and called toward the upstairs. She called twice. "He never hears—I'll get him." At the door she paused. "Listen, it sure was nice of you to get him home the other night. I appreciate it."

"Oh, that's nothin. He jus need somebody to poke him, sort of, or he forget what he doin."

Brian came into the kitchen, and he and Martha looked at each other across the table. Martha said formally, "I just stop round to see how you doing. Is your momma better?"

"Yeah, she's better," Brian said. He looked over his shoulder toward the living room and saw her chair empty. "I guess she's gone to the store. She started taking her pills again, and she ain't drinking now."

"I surely am glad," Martha said. They stood there awkwardly, and then Martha said, "You want to come out? Me and Melvita and Dwayne, we jus walkin round. We could go feed yo dog or somethin."

"O.K.," Brian said and he followed her out the door. Outside the screen, he stopped and shouted back: "Hey, Eve! I'm going out awhile. I'll be back."

"Hey, Brian," Dwayne said.

"Hey, Dwayne. Hi, Melvita." He looked at them and away, shy, but pleased to be with the three of them all together. Somehow he'd never connected them—they were three different people he talked to in different places.

"Brian want to go feed his dog," Martha said.

"You still messin with that dog?" Melvita said.

Dwayne said, "You ain't never showed him to me."

"You didn't want to come," Brian said.

"Aw, that be all over now. Come on!" They walked over to old Maisie's and hung on the fence, and Brian noticed the curtain twitching more than usual. The door opened and the quavering voice shouted: "Go on! Get away from here now!"

"Look out, Melvita!" Dwayne laughed. "Ole Maisie goin put the eye on you! Come on, girl, you and me goin to sell Girl Scout cookies, make a pile of money!" Melvita giggled, and they went off down the street.

"It's just me, ma'am," Brian called to the old lady. They heard her mumbling to herself, and then she closed the door.

"Let's go round to that little porch you fix up," Martha said. "I didn hardly see it by daylight, just by lightnin light! So everythin be all right at yo house now?"

"Yeah, I guess. We'll manage." He looked up at her. "How about you? Did you tell your mother or anyone? You know, about the baby?"

"Oh, lordy, I forget! I didn see you yesterday and I clean forget! I ain't goin have no baby."

"How come?"

Martha hooted. "I just ain't, that be all. I ain't pregnant."

"You sorry?"

"You crazy boy! You think I want to give my momma and daddy all that worry? Course I ain't sorry."

"Well . . . I am, sort of. It'd be nice to have a baby."

"Yeah. It be nice. Someday, but not now."

"You're going to be in school like always, huh?"

"Sure! Goin to be in school, be in high school, then I goin to be someone. You, too!" She kicked a broken bottle in the yard. "Somethin got to grow in this here garden of broken glass!"

BESTSELLERS FROM
LAUREL-LEAF LIBRARY

**Outstanding Laurel-Leaf Fiction
for Young Adult Readers**

☐ **A LITTLE DEMONSTRATION OF AFFECTION**
  Elizabeth Winthrop $1.25
A 15-year-old girl and her older brother find themselves turning
to each other to share their deepest emotions.

☐ **M.C. HIGGINS THE GREAT**
  Virginia Hamilton $1.25
Winner of the Newbery Medal, the National Book Award and
the Boston Globe-Horn Book Award, this novel follows M.C.
Higgins' growing awareness that both choice and action lie
within his power.

☐ **PORTRAIT OF JENNIE**
  Robert Nathan $1.25
Robert Nathan interweaves touching and profound portraits of
all his characters with one of the most beautiful love stories
ever told.

☐ **THE MEAT IN THE SANDWICH**
  Alice Bach $1.25
Mike Lefcourt dreams of being a star athlete, but when hockey
season ends, Mike learns that victory and defeat become
hopelessly mixed up.

☐ **Z FOR ZACHARIAH**
  Robert C. O'Brien $1.25
This winner of an Edgar Award from the Mystery Writers of
America portrays a young girl who was the only human being
left alive after nuclear doomsday—or so she thought.